AGNISAKSHI

AGNISAKSHI
FIRE, MY WITNESS

Lalithambika Antharjanam

Translated from Malayalam by
Vasanthi Sankaranarayanan

Edited by
Mini Krishnan

OXFORD
UNIVERSITY PRESS

OXFORD
UNIVERSITY PRESS

Oxford University Press is a department of the University of Oxford.
It furthers the University's objective of excellence in research, scholarship,
and education by publishing worldwide. Oxford is a registered trademark of
Oxford University Press in the UK and in certain other countries

Published in India by
Oxford University Press
YMCA Library Building, 1 Jai Singh Road, New Delhi 110 001, India

First published in Malayalam in 1976
First English translation published by Kerala Sahitya Akademi in 1980
Published in Malayalam by DC Books, Kottayam, Kerala, in 2010
This edition published by Oxford University Press India
in arrangement with DC Books in 2015

ISBN-13: 978-0-19-945700-7
ISBN-10: 0-19-945700-X

Typeset in Trump Mediaeval LT Std 9.5/14.5
by Sai Graphic Design, New Delhi 110 055
Printed in India by Sapra Brothers, New Delhi 110 092

To my father,
who taught me the virtues of
Truth, Tolerance, and Integrity

Contents

Author's Note[*]

When I present this novel, *Agnisakshi*, to my readers, I wish to
add a few words as supplemental information. You may take it as
a friendly conversation between the readers and the novelist. I am
not a novelist. To imagine the full form and structure of a great
literary genre like a novel and to fulfil such a serious job with
dedication—I did not have the convenience during my youth or
middle age. Women of Kerala from ordinary families, who function as mothers, household heads, and hostesses, find it difficult
to take up writing as a full-time job. If they get some leisure time,
they write some small pieces—short stories, poems, articles. In
between, I experimented and wrote substantial portions of one
or two novels and abandoned them. Thus time passed. Now, at
sixty-seven, I have neither the desire, nor the arrogance that I am
capable of writing a critically satisfactory novel. Even so, destiny
has made me place before you a small book in the form of this
novel. Even to me, it is not clear how this came about. The term
'fate' has been repeated in this book on several occasions. What
exactly is 'fate'?

Does it consist of events and experiences that we are forced to
face, unable to change them? Or are they persuasions of karma,
which lead us in an imponderable manner? I have never believed
in fate. In fact, I believed that there is nothing that human intelli-

[*] Originally prepared as the epilogue to this novel, we decided to present this piece as the late author's note.

gence and will power cannot achieve. But I frankly admit that this book was not created through my ability alone. The story is not based purely on imagination. Usually, I only write stories based on what I have seen, heard, or experienced and have touched me deeply. I have paid attention to various events where the truth turns out to be stranger than imagination. But there is no other narrative which touched my heart with such compassion and no other narration that refused to fade however much I resisted it, no other narration that mingled so strongly with my imagination; after a long time, it broke the barriers of time and flowed forcefully through me. For a long time, this story lay like a wound in my mind. In solitary moments, it brought tears to my eyes. I had firmly decided that whatever happened, I would never write about this, never ever. How weak human decisions are! I admit failure; as nothing can be hidden from my readers, let me tell you that story.

There were three stages in the creation of this book.

First of all, the great task of producing the seed. That happened in the month of May in 1962, at a pilgrimage centre in Uttar Pradesh. There, quite accidentally, I met a woman ascetic. She was a Malayali. She wore a saffron-coloured khaddar *mundu*, blouse, and shawl. She had shaved her head. We talked a great deal about the ashrams, sages, and ways of life in that place. I had heard that one of my old friends, a social worker, now a renunciate, lived somewhere around there. I asked this woman whether she knew my friend. Suddenly, she grew pale. Recognizing her special facial features, I too turned pale. That ascetic was the same woman about whom I had enquired. The changes wrought in us over twenty years! Having recognized me, without uttering a word, she picked up a vessel and went down to the banks of the Ganga.

Looking at that glowing figure and its shadow, I stood stunned for a long time. (Because it was afternoon, the shadow behind her looked longer than usual.) I felt very sad. I remembered the stories of several women who had forgotten or rejected family life and entered the sphere of social service and finally sought solace in renunciation. I had come to the conclusion that such sacred stories should only be stored in our minds, and not written down. That silent tragedy tormented me. In the end, I forgot it. Thus, seven or eight years passed with that tragic story buried in my subconscious.

Secondly, in May 1970 at Trivandrum, in one of my weak moments, I promised that I would write a serialized story for a radio broadcast. We had to provide the title of the story before we began to write. I remembered the name of a short story I had written, probably in 1945, of a revolutionary social worker. The title was 'Prasadam'. When the heat of the revolution died down a bit, the malignance that she received from her co-workers as well as those who opposed her wearied her, making her seek solace in prayer. This was the story. At that time, some people had opined that I should make it into a novel. The theme was a well-known one. So, I suggested the name 'Prasadam' to the broadcasting centre. Ten sections, each section to be read in fifteen minutes. I wrote each of them, one at a time, and submitted them. Only when I heard a great part of the script being read did I suspect that it was not the story that I had planned to write, but the story which I had carefully hidden in my mind that had now leapt out without my knowledge. When the programme was relayed, I received a great deal of praise. But I gave up the idea of publishing a novel in the same form. I even decided that it need not be published at all. Five or six years passed.

Then, most unexpectedly, last May, the editor of *Mathrubhumi Weekly* requested me to write a novel for the weekly. At first I was stunned. I became anxious. In this old age, a novel? My right hand ached, my eyesight had dimmed—no, no, I'll tell them that I can't do it. Then I felt, why not try? This too could be fate's command. There were unfinished scripts of some old novels, scribbled in notebooks. I took them out, wiped the dust off them, and chose this one. The narrative was like a child lying pressed to the bosom of the mother, which could not be plucked and thrown aside. I changed the structure. I untied the contents and rebuilt them. The story turned out to be completely new. I began living it. The method of storytelling depends on the subject and it emerged on its own. It must have taken that shape to enable me to shorten and compress the history of a long era. The first fifteen chapters from Thankam Nair's perspective, and the second fifteen from that of Devi Bahen—altogether, thirty chapters. I wanted to write it in two sections. But for many reasons, I had to finish the second section in three chapters. Because of that, the portrait of Devi Bahen might have turned out to be pale and weak. I crave your forgiveness!

I did mention that this story is not purely a product of my imagination. Nor is it, at the same time, any one person's profile or biography. Nor did I write this novel to document the history of the woman ascetic whom I met at the *tirthaghat* or someone else. Perhaps the emotions she roused in me, along with the influence of the times, must have persuaded the untold story to take another shape on its own. A realistic depiction of life can never be art. When such a depiction merges with the heart and takes another birth, it becomes art. The form of imagination, which accepts along with it the outline of the story, nurturing it and giving it life, will be reflected in the creative process. I had thought that using some stories which I had experienced or known of, this novel should act as a diary of notes of the social and political changes that had taken place during forty long years. Even though it was written about the circumstances that a particular community faced, a hint of the general issues faced in the social life of those times can be found in this book. Sumitrananda, who is introduced through three names—Tethi Edathi, Devaki Manampalli, and Devi Bahen—reveals three faces of the life led by the women of the previous generation. Resorting to another way of life, thereby becoming an example of the modern young woman, Thankam Nair becomes the narrator as well as the witness of this history. Viewed from another perspective, the writer's conscience might have changed paths for convenience sake and made Thankam appear like this. I had always been very moved by the emotions of children born of the outside-community relationships of the Namboodiris. They were unable to approach, or touch their fathers, or eat with them. They could not even care for them when they fell ill. They were never treated as children of the clan.

Unni Ettan is a creation of my own imagination. I have never met a man like him. Even though he is very conservative and regressive, I respect the truth of the ideal that he represents. But he has to bear the punishment for forgetting the principle that married life should include caring for one's wife and having children through her; not merely upholding the ritualistic aspect of being united in the presence of a sacred fire.

Aphan Namboodiri, Ettan's mother, the grandmother obsessed with the idea of pollution through touch which can be removed only by cleaning oneself with water, the insane young aunt—all these people were there with me in my day-to-day life. I have witnessed the older Aphans throwing water jugs at mad younger aunts and wounding them. I have seen these ignored wives going at night to their husband's mistress's house, umbrella in one hand and the edge of the new mundu in the other, shrieking and creating embarassing scenes. I have also witnessed young, unruly boys yelling 'sex-crazy' at them and pursuing them.

I have even seen elderly women limping to the pond and immersing themselves a thousand and eight times, still unable to decide whether it was done properly or not. I know of the noblest of Brahmins who, when enraged, abuse and curse in the grossest manner. None of them exist now. But, even now, there are new types who imitate them in other ways.

Life is like the Ganga and the Himalaya. Even though in the beginning a pilgrimage to these places seems boring and fraught with difficulties, towards the end, it gives us a sense of bliss. This book, which I planned as two sections and thirty chapters, now condensed to eighteen chapters might seem flawed. You must forgive me for that. If this helps the women of the new generation to have a better understanding of their counterparts of the older generation, while persuading the older generation to analyse themselves, and other people to examine the tears and dreams of a bygone age, it will suffice.

It is the sympathy I feel for the suffering human souls that has always prompted me to write creatively. The ideas that are warmed in one's imagination will gradually begin to glow, flame, and move. They accept another birth and life. I think that the chemistry, which changes blood into breast milk, is the same one that makes the truth into art in one's imagination ... If I am able to transfer a portion of the emotion that I had experienced while writing this novel to my readers, I will feel blessed.

LALITHAMBIKA ANTHARJANAM
1976

Translator's Note

In the year 2010 when I applied for a Charles Wallace Scholarship, I had to name and describe a project which I wished to pursue. The scholarship was for the translation of an Indian-language book into English. Mini Krishnan, who has been a mentor and guide, suggested that I retranslate *Agnisakshi* (1976) by Lalithambika Antharjanam, which I had done long ago for Kerala Sahitya Akademi (1980).

At first, I did not find the idea overly thrilling. For me, the challenge and enthusiasm in translation did not lie in walking a road already taken. I usually translate works which have touched me through their narrative, ideology, structure, or language. *Agnisakshi* had appealed to me greatly when I translated it, but that was over thirty years ago. I had first read the book when it was serialized in *Mathrubhumi Weekly*, at which time I had found the language poetic and unusual and the contents emotionally moving. It was my first attempt at translation and I was lucky that the author herself entrusted this task to me.

By the time I began my translation, the book had won all the literary awards in India, including the National Sahitya Akademi and the Kerala Sahitya Akademi awards for the best book of the year. I greatly admired Lalithambika, with whom I had already started a dialogue through letters. Her affection for me revealed through her letters made me feel that I had to do this translation. Looking back on that period, I feel that I was Thankam Nair and she, Tethikutty Antharjanam (characters from the book). I felt it was a great honour, and as a much younger person who had not previously attempted to translate anything at all, I had some doubts about my capability to fulfil the job. However, with great faith and optimism, I began the translation and finished it within six months. If I remember correctly, there was no serious criticism against the translation and the book was printed in 1980. I did not look forward to a repeat performance of the same work.

Mini explained to me the advantages of translating the same book a second time. It was the only novel of an iconic Malayalam author who was no more and a classic of Malayalam literature deserved a reinterpretation through a fresh translation. It had been made into a film by the same name by the well-known director Shyamaprasad and had won the best film award from the Kerala government and the central government. The era recalled in this book is a span of post- and pre-Independent years, altogether forty years, which is a significant period in the history of India and Kerala in particular. It also depicted the social customs prevalent in Kerala in the early part of the twentieth century, especially in the Namboodiri community, and came from a woman author. Two of the main characters in the novel are women, each in her own way trying to break away from the conservative and antiquated traditions that existed at that time to find their own freedom, and to thus carve out new lives for themselves. They could be called the early revolutionaries who sought female empowerment in Kerala.

I began, reluctantly, to see Mini's point of view. Suddenly, I did a 360-degree turn and felt I was destined to translate this book once again. Was it the force Antharjanam herself called 'fate'? Now, on the eve of this book going to press, I feel it is a 'niyogam', which in Malayalam means 'entrustment'. Often, while I was going through the exercise of editing along with Mini, who literally forced me to reinterpret the contents, I could feel the presence of Antharjanam herself requesting me to do this job. I felt that I would be honouring her charismatic presence in Malayalam literature, especially in the early women's writing of Kerala through retranslation and reinterpretation. More than a hundred years have passed after her birth, and this would be a befitting gift to a generous and creative person like her. I also feel that I am the right person to do this translation, having gone through the exercise once before. Since my paternal grandfather was a Namboodiri, not only do I know the customs and habits of the Namboodiris, but having lived in its shadow, I have close connections with that tradition.

Apart from the literary, political, and social significance of this book, Mini felt that it would be a landmark in my translation career. When I translated the book over thirty years ago, I was a novice. Since then, the art of translation as well as my own knowledge and experience and technique have changed and developed. Translation as an art form has gained more importance in India, and its theory and practice have become highly visible, more widely discussed, and popular. As such, this translation would be a commentary on the modern and ever-changing techniques of translation and experiments in it. Thus, Mini convinced me about the legitimacy of a retranslation.

I applied for the scholarship, received it, and was attached to the University of East Anglia, renowned for its translation department. I began my work on this new translation in March 2011 and completed it by December 2011. I did the translation, but it is Mini, through her superior skills in editing, who has polished and refined the language. The changes in the language of the translation are a credit to her experience and knowledge in this field. To her, I owe a very big thank you. I leave the readers to pass judgement or critique the book in translation.

What I was not prepared for was the change in my own mental make-up towards the book. In 1980, I was thrilled that such a well-

known book was to be translated by me and I never questioned the
language, contents, or ideology of the author. There was also an
element of hero worship in my attitude to Lalithambika and her
literary product. I had not delved deep into the subliminal mes-
sages that come through the book. In other words, I accepted the
book without questioning either the contents or the language. At
that time, my ideological stances, especially on feminism, were
unclear and shaky. In 2011, with my new understanding of literary
merit as well the political and social ideologies, I looked at the
same work with a more critical eye. My attitude changed and with
it my translatorial approach. I think it would be dishonest to not
explain this new critical attitude to my readers, so I have tried to
put into words my own estimation and analysis of *Agnisakshi* as
a literary product based on this new understanding. This, I hasten
to add, does not in any way diminish the importance of the book
as a literary work, or my admiration for the author and her work;
instead it adds a new dimension to its contents from a feminist
perspective.

I take inspiration in critiquing this book from the appendix the
author wrote, which we have positioned as the Author's Note in
this book. She has admitted that she was new to writing a novel.
I wondered why Antharjanam stopped with eighteen chapters.
Why not seventeen or twenty? My own deduction is that it had
something to do with eighteen being an important and auspicious
number in the Hindu tradition:

The Mahabharatam war lasted eighteen days and the epic itself
is divided into eighteen books or parvas.

The *Bhagavad Gita*[1] has eighteen cantos.

---

[1] Also known as the *Gita*, it is Sree Krishna's advice to Arjuna before
the commencement of the eighteen-day war between the Pandavas and
the Kauravas.

There are eighteen *Puranas* according to the Hindu tradition. The martial disciplines of Kerala comprise eighteen stances or *adavus*.

The eighteenth step, as in the *patinettam pati* of Sabarimala, an important piligrimage centre, is the one which supposedly gives a person release from worldly bonds and a vision of the ultimate. Antharjanam, who was aware of all these significances, chose to stop at the eighteenth chapter hoping that in spite of condensing the novel it would have the desired creative and emotional impact on readers. She did not leave any notes or jottings for us to cross-check. From the above, I dare to suggest that Antharjanam felt guilty for not fulfilling her original plan for the novel and was hoping for expiation by stopping it at an auspicious number. This may or may not be true and is pure guesswork on my part.

But my analysis of the book starts from the condensation of the book into eighteen chapters and, therefore, any information arising from intelligent deduction or mere curiosity becomes important for my conclusions that follow.

Has the novel suffered structurally from this compression? In my opinion, it has. As Antharjanam guessed, this compression resulted in insufficient importance being given to the character or tragic tale of Sumitrananda. Apart from that, it destabilized the structure of the novel as a whole. One feels that the book ends abruptly and leaves something unsaid. That leads us to the question: who is Antharjanam's heroine? There appear to be two—Thankam Nair and Tethikutty. Why did she pack importance, intensity, and depth into Thankam Nair's tale and truncate Sumitrananda's? Antharjanam has explained in the appendix about her sympathy for children born from Namboodiris' liaisons. So, she did not find it difficult to describe Thankam Nair and her plight. Antharjanam could afford to show compassion, tinged with condescension, as it was in line with her liberal humanistic attitude towards a woman who did not belong to her community. She has also narrated the tragic tale of Sumitrananda, but the style is almost like that of a didactic, verbose prose report. We are not allowed to share the agony and vulnerability of this character, a true revolutionary of that time. Therefore, she emerges as a cardboard character and not a lively one.

Did Antharjanam do it consciously, or was it an accident, or was it creative disability? My own deduction is that a responsible and highly creative author like her could not have done it accidentally. Even though she may not be aware of it, this neglect of Sumitrananda's character—the unfortunate, restless, wandering figure who never attains reassurance, satisfaction, or release, almost an outcaste from the traditional values of Namboodiris— was not accidental. Though Antharjanam shows outward signs of sympathy for this unfortunate woman, the subliminal message that comes to us is that she personally did not approve of the path Tethi took to achieve freedom. Even Thankam, who was very close to Tethi, and loved her and understood her dilemma, voices this opinion. Again, Tethi had to move from revolution—challenging the orthodoxy—to *seva* by becoming Gandhi's disciple and later to renunciation. This, according to Antharjanam, shows her restlessness and lack of clear-cut ideas on the path she has to take. Antharjanam is unable to forgive Tethi, even when she assumes *sannyasam*, or be sympathetic to her vulnerabilities, though in a general sense, she admires the act of renunciation. That is why she binds Tethi emotionally to her past and makes her accept the husband she had abandoned as her true spiritual guru. Antharjanam makes Tethi/Sumitranandan admit that she has not achieved liberation from her past, that is, her husband. In other words, she is a failure. In the end, only when Thankam's son prostrates before her and pleads silently to accept him as her son, does she, Tethi, get some sort of release. In one stroke, Antharjanam has re-established her faith in the sanctity of family, marriage, and motherhood. She seems to be saying that no revolution against these traditions will last, particularly an inner search undertaken by a woman. This, from a woman's perspective, is one of the major flaws in Antharjanam's characterization. Probably, that is why when social reformers of the Namboodiri community, like V.T. Bhattathirppad accepted Kuriyedath Tatri[2] as the forerunner of all later reforms, Antharjanam in her own short story, *'Pratikaradevatha'* (Revenge Herself), remonstrates with the ghost of Tatri for having embarked on the path of revenge and advises her that she should have waited for social reformers to take up her cause. From this instance too it is clear that Antharjanam is not for revolutions which affect the solidity of the Namboodiri tradition, causing women to question the ideals of family, marriage, and motherhood. So, while on the face of it Antharjanam's novel is about two women who were oppressed by the restrictions of tradition and sought freedom from these shackles, both her heroines do not gain any self-fulfilment or satisfaction from their attempts to change their lives. This has convinced me that while Antharjanam wrote from a woman's point of view, she could not completely free herself from the norms of patriarchy.

Lalithambika was a product of her times. She was a freedom fighter who gave a great deal of importance to women's emancipation. She was against the injustices and ills perpetrated on women,

---

[2] A Namboodiri woman tried for being unfaithful to her husband and declared an outcaste. The historic trial took place in 1905. In the course of the trial, she managed to indict sixty-four prominent upper-caste men, caused them to lose caste stating that they were partners in her crime, and should therefore be accorded the same punishment. This is considered the beginning of a movement among the Namboodiris to empower women and community reform.

especially by the Namboodiri community. She tried to protest against these through her actions and her literary writings. But, she was a traditionalist in many ways. She believed in the sanctity of marriage, the strength of a family in the social system, the power of renunciation, and the respect for traditional rituals and values. Though she was a member of the Communist Party, she could not reconcile herself with women's freedom in its ultimate sense, against the social fabric of observance of traditional values, such as fidelity to marriage and family. So my conclusion is that Antharjanam could idealize women's freedom only if they kept within the existing social fabric.

The story revolves around the sister-in-law, Tethi, who leaves home, and through three stages in her life: Devaki Manampalli, a social worker; Devi Bahen, a follower of Gandhiji; and finally Sumitrananda, a renunciate. And Unni, Thankam Nair's brother and Tethikutty's husband. On the surface, the narrative seems to be centred on the two women, Thankam Nair and Tethikutty Antharjanam. It is their story and history. However, from the way the characters and their actions are described, Unni's character appears larger than life and overshadows those of the two women characters.

When I read the book for retranslation, I felt that it was not just the book and Antharjanam as the author, but even her two female characters, who seemed to be justifying the choices that Unni made in spite of all his shortcomings. They both loved him to the very end. I do not exactly know why I didn't feel this way when I first translated the book. All I can say in support of my reanalysis of the contents is that my awareness of feminist ideology has become clearer, and that I feel that Lalithambika's idea of revolution probably belonged to a middle path wherein revolution does not demand a complete change, but asks only for a partial one. Compared to women authors of her time, Antharjanam can, with the exception of Saraswathi Amma, probably be treated as an unusual and innovative author who strove to bring about ideas of female empowerment. But her hesitation to really challenge the old patriarchal value system and seek a complete change is quite evident in this novel.

Though the backdrop to this story is the traditional society of Kerala and the Indian National Freedom struggle that was raging all over India then, we do not get any substantial or poignant details of the struggle itself and how it affected people and their lives, except in one chapter where a brave young boy was brutally killed by the police for raising the national flag and shouting national slogans. Wherever there are descriptions of events relating to this important event of India's freedom struggle, the language becomes one of reportage and not that of story or history. Since the entire narrative draws poignancy from the background, the language loses its literary quality and turns into didactic prose.

It is important to note that Antharjanam does not make any mention of the struggle of the lower castes to gain freedom, equality, and respect from their local masters or the colonial ones. It is almost as though they did not exist at all. Antharjanam's partiality to fair-skinned people is also evident from some of the descriptions. There is no political awareness of the subordination of the lower castes or the dominance and sense of superiority of the white men over Indians which was one of the main reasons for the revolt for freedom. It is all blotted out of the novel; a serious omission.

In the later chapters, the language tends to be very ordinary and preachy. It loses its lyrical quality and turns prosaic. Overall, there is a tendency to stress traditional values and religious rituals. The ideas of 'fate' and 'renunciation' take strong roots in the book and become oppressive which, on the whole, weakens the strength and beauty of the language.

It would not be correct to end this note without mentioning the strengths of the novel. Even though the language is patchy, there are passages where it rises to poetic prose and emotional poignancy. Were we to take the novel as a tale of the love between a brother and a sister, it moves us intensely. Both the characters, Unni and Thankam, become alive when their relationship is explored. The only time Unni shows some courage is when he pleads with Aphan Namboodiri to allow Thankam to continue her studies. Again, the relationship between Aphan Namboodiri and Unni is described with unusual poignancy. In spite of being a task-master and dictator, Aphan Namboodiri held his nephew Unni in high regard, a man who was in every way different from him. Likewise, Unni's emotional dilemma in seeking Aphan's approval to retrieve his wife, Tethikutty, is intense. He alone knew Aphan Namboodiri's strengths and weaknesses and chose not to exploit the same. Instead, Unni chose to suffer silently. As an isolated event, this sacrifice has its own appeal and poignancy. In fact, he showed compassion to all, including the mad younger aunt, except his own wife, Tethikutty. He expected her to understand him completely and play the role of the traditional wife. Another instance of Unni's strength of character is when he refuses a second marriage, despite strong persuasion by Aphan and his mother. In his own way, he was faithful to Tethikutty. But it was not enough for a woman like her. As feminists, we have to question this kind of spirituality, bordering on selfishness.

Another aspect in which this novel is remarkable is the way Antharjanam has described the ins and outs of a traditional Namboodiri household. It is truly an insider's perspective and has a quaint, charming quality to it, especially when she describes the rituals of *Thiruvathira* and the fire, which is considered the most important of the five elements. She has also been able to weave in ideas from other faiths, such as the story of Prometheus from

Greek mythology and the Christian view of Madonna, without losing the spontaneity and flow of the narrative.

Her language itself is unusual. She is one of the earliest to use a single-word or single-phrase sentence, creating a resonance of their own. Though the language is not even, there are passages which give us a glimpse of the poetic and lyrical quality of Malayalam.

To sum up, Lalithambika's is an extraordinary and unusual period novel. As I write this note critiquing certain aspects of her novel, I hope that Antharjanam will forgive me for my frankness, which does not in any way diminish my respect for her or her creativity.

VASANTHI SANKARANARAYANAN

Introduction

Herstory, not History—Reading *Agnisakshi* in the Early Twenty-first Century

Agnisakshi, Lalithambika Antharjanam's only novel, appeared relatively late in her long and illustrious writing career, which stretched from the late 1920s to the end of the 1980s. While she had begun her career as a poet, it was her short stories that made her a presence in the field of modern Malayalam literature. Along with her brilliant contemporary K. Saraswathi Amma, Lalithambika decisively broadened and deepened a new critical tradition of literary writing in Malayalam, that of women's anti-patriarchal writing in the decades of the mid-twentieth century. The first generation of modern, educated women grappled with the question of gender and the role of individuated women in a society in the throes of social change and political upheaval. Even as a young woman, Lalithambika identified her writing as fully immersed in and shaped by her engagement with these wider processes. A friend remembered her words to him, 'Some unnamable discontent, terrible desire, is constantly gnawing [at] my heart. A feeling that God had entrusted me with some noble responsibility, that I had not yet fulfilled even the smallest part of it' (Abdulkhadar 1946: 88–9).[1]

---

[1] All translations are mine unless mentioned otherwise.

The readers of *Agnisakshi* will surely find the two female protagonists of the novel—Devaki Manampalli and Thankam Nair—echoing precisely these sentiments. It is also possible to understand why both Lalithambika Antharjanam and K. Saraswathi Amma wrote their only novels rather later in their careers—when one takes notice of the sense of mission that was characteristic of many women of their generation. For their novels seem to embody their intellectual engagement with discourse of modern gender, which cleaved the world neatly into the home and the public—the alternate philosophies of gender that they were groping towards in and through their short stories. Some of the early sketches towards *Agnisakshi* are to be found in some of Lalithambika's early short stories like '*Maralakal*', '*Prasadam*', '*Udayathinu Nere*', and '*Mulappalinte Manam*'.

However, in *Agnisakshi*, this alternate philosophy of gender is presented in and through an alternate history. Lalithambika presents to another generation of female readers a slice of twentieth-century history—that of upper-caste educated Malayali women. She gives an account of the historical experiences of upper-caste Malayali women of the twentieth century exposed to community reformism and modern education, seeking to link women of different generations through bonds of understanding, representing their past to them. The different trajectories taken by upper-caste women in early twentieth-century Malayali society in their search for self-fulfilment are unravelled through the memories of the two central protagonists—Devaki Manampalli and Thankam Nair. In the preface to the 1980 edition, Lalithambika says, '[I will be satisfied] ... if this serves to help women of the younger generation to understand their mothers and grandmothers; [if it will help] ... members of the older generation to conduct a self-examination; and others, to bring together and study the tears and dreams of a past time' (1980: 9).

This reinforces the claim of *Agnisakshi* to be regarded as a 'her-story' of elite women, for sure, but still one largely ignored even now by mainstream accounts of the past. It is difficult to express in summary both the enormous achievements of this generation and their unspeakably unjust marginalization, their passionate involvement in the shaping of modern Malayali society, and the hurdles they had to overcome. Lalithambika's generation deserved to be called the 'first-generation feminists' because they advanced claims, engaged in polemics, and constructed alternate visions of gender, all on behalf of the putative collective identity 'Women'. However, it is surely proof of the male-centredness of dominant accounts of our history that they faded from the official histori-cal record and public memory almost entirely. In fact, this was already the state of affairs by the 1970s, when *Agnisakshi* was written. Considering this, the novel is surely a bridge between elite Malayali women of the early twentieth century and their counterparts of the present. More important perhaps is her obser-vation (as given above) that it may also be an instrument towards critical self-reflexivity and reflection for both generations.

The early twentieth century saw two different life trajectories opening up to elite Malayali women. The most frequently dis-cussed and endorsed path was that of the educated modern house-wife, a role highly praised by emergent social and community reformists as pivotal to the shaping of modern society. The other, less discussed and frequently criticized and contested path was of public life, as self-sacrificing social and political activist. The great tragedy of elite Malayali women, as Lalithambika saw it, was that these paths were not merely different, but actually cut-off from each other. Devaki Manampalli and Thankam Nair traverse these mutually exclusive paths, and their increasing distance forms the core of the pathos of their story. It is worth noting that the novel presents this divergence as breaking up an original unity, an intimate friendship, characterized by complete openness to each other, and close knowledge of each other's internal lives. It makes impossible the keeping of a promise, made in a crucial moment before their separation—to maintain this unity by sharing their children—that is, the dream of building a bond *between* women, not restricted by the boundaries of patrifocal families.

Devaki and Thankam come to occupy spaces they had not originally desired, and somehow ranged in opposition to one another. As they individuate in the tumultuous social and political context of the early twentieth century, Devaki desires modern conjugal companionship and motherhood; while Thankam's ambitions are focused on active public life. But it is Thankam who becomes the housewife and Devaki, the public activist. In the course of their lives, they are isolated from each other and are more or less absorbed in the pursuit of their own narrow goals. However, these trajectories never absorb them fully, and now and then 'unnameable discontents' disturb the normal flow of lives as chance events. Thankam recognizes as comfortable and peaceful but dulling, her life as the satisfied wife of a well-placed official and the mother of a son, 'I was beginning a new life. My son's arrival. Husband's promotion. New duties in life. Immersed in all this, [I] ... did not feel time go by. I was happy, contented. Then there was no time to think of old relationships' (1980: 92). She admits that the events in the world outside, where the nationalist struggle was beginning to climax, had little impact on her, 'All this had on me only the effect of a detective novel' (1980: 92). But, witnessing the scene of a nationalist demonstration being brutally broken up by the British police, from the balcony of her safe secure home, an apartment not only well-defined and limited a space, but also raised high above the ground, she is plagued with guilt, 'How weak am I! How wretched! Why did I not run down into that crowd, why did I not say, "I am also an Indian. I am also with you ... Take me with you, sister"' (1980: 92). Recognizing the woman leading the demonstration to be Devaki, Thankam enquires about her whereabouts, only to realize that their spaces were not only separate, but also in opposition to each other.

As for Devaki, she suppresses her desire for modern conjugality and plunges into public life. Her long public career is marked by restless wandering from one role to another—first as a social reformer, then as a Gandhian political activist in the anticolonial struggle, and later as a Gandhian social activist in independent India. A series of events leading to the failure of sexual self-disciplining and mutual trust between the inmates of her ashram shocks her out of the life and beliefs of a social activist into ever-severe isolation as an ascetic. This, however, prompts self-reflection and re-evaluation of her beliefs, precisely those that she had suppressed:

> Even the word 'desire' used to drive her into a fury. But did she manage to hate the creative urge inherent in all living beings? She looked around the ashram with a sigh: disciples, daughters, Mataji, Mother. Yes, all of Woman's dearest wishes must anchor at this shore in order to be fulfilled. She wanted to cover the entire living world in a kiss, to call aloud, 'My children!' But no one wants a Mother, they want a Guru, a Yogini ... (1980: 132–3)

It is obvious at this point that this twentieth-century her-story of elite Malayali Womanhood—found implicated in the wider project of individual self-fulfilment—is a critical one. Through the critical component, it distances itself from the commonplace view of this period—echoed in countless popular accounts and textbooks—that it was an era of 'liberation' for Malayali women. In fact, it is precisely the discontents of such a project of liberation that are highlighted here. The spaces which female individuals in early to mid-twentieth-century Malayali society—represented by the two chief protagonists—could occupy were also spaces of the 'hard individual'—with the upper case 'I'. The critique of the philosophy of the Individual is a perennial theme in Lalithambika's work. It needs to be remembered that the ideal of the rational, competitive, self-sufficient, productive Individual in the exclusive sense was central to many of the dominant projects of social and community reform of these times. Many of her short stories relate the tragedies that ultimately befall such individuals, who pursue chosen life-projects, focusing mainly on narrow personal trajectories, and in the process, refuse or ignore their social bonds. Their inward-looking seems to sever them from others. In other words, they are negligent of what is made to figure as the more important social responsibility—the forging of harmonious, non-violent, tolerant, equitable social relationships.

In many of Lalithambika's short stories, Individuals are ultimately made to see their efforts as fruitless labour. Three important aspects may be identified in this critique. The most commonly stressed aspect is the demonstration of the *impossibility* of the pursuits so steadfastly adhered to by such protagonists. It is as though one *must*, one *will*, be entangled in social bonds at one point or another. A second aspect is linked to the role of social ties in giving the Individual a sense of independence and mobility. It reveals that what underlies such feeling is the strength and support given by the Individual's social ties. Thirdly, such individuality is seen to trap the Individual in an illusion of self-fulfilment and even power. When this illusion fades, the person is left emptied of emotional resources to fall back upon.

A careful reading of *Agnisakshi* would reveal the elaboration of all three aspects in Lalithambika's critique in it. They undergird her reading of the past of elite Malayali women. The entry of Malayali women of this generation into public activism as well as their integration into the modern family as domestic managers are seen to have led women into the spaces of the 'hard' Individual, locking them away from each other into seemingly watertight social boxes. It is asserted that this has denied them self-fulfilment, despite social recognition and personal happiness. It is faulted to have obstructed the formation of a collectivity of women based on sharing. The imagining of this collectivity is never explicit, but remains an abiding presence throughout. It seems highly informed by Lalithambika's reimagining motherhood as elaborated in *'Mulappalinte Manam'*, in which the figure of Ammini Amma is not corralled within domestic space. *Agnisakshi* advances a passionate vision of motherhood that does not shun public life, and of public life that does not shun motherhood, but rather draws energy from it. It is as if Devaki's and Thankam's reunion *could not but* happen, as though their mutual separation was a forced intervention in Nature *that cannot but* be impermanent—and that is precisely why 'unnameable discontents' continue to plague them in their busy, seemingly fulfilled careers. The reunion of Thankam and Devaki, so it seems, would bring the sundered halves together, 'Devaki Manamballi has no escape from Thankam Nair. We are the two faces of an era. The new generation has two mothers, will you not accept our children?' (Antharjanam 1980: 99). Thankam brings to Devaki her son, and Devaki presents Thankam's granddaughter with her *thali*, the symbol of her immense self-control, sacrifice, and steadfastness. The two exchange what they consider to be the most valuable achievements of their lives. This exchange is celebrated as a moment of communion, which seems to imply the effacement of boundaries through the use of the metaphor of mothers' milk aflow, 'It was as if breast-milk was flowing from all of Nature's body—the end of tapas—a new era was being born' (1980: 151).

It is worth noting though at this very moment, the limitations of Lalithambika's re-vision are also evident. The commingling of spaces, which the two protagonists seek to effect, the recreation of wholeness hitherto prevented, it seems, is quite impossible. For, though a commingling of spaces is sought, what seems to be happening is merely an exchange. The tension is obvious: individuality is by no means unseated.

Perhaps the self-reflexivity that the Malayali woman reader of the early twenty-first century may gain from the novel lies here. It urges us to turn away from the male-stream story of the 'liberation' of (at least the elite) Malayali woman in the twentieth century. It drives home the realization that women cannot come together unless they breach the narrow socio-spatial boxes which they are locked into structurally. And besides, reject the still-dominant practice of placing the domestic and public in opposition to each other. It is important to realize the full political import of this reminder in the present, for these are times in which 'women's empowerment' has become a keyword everywhere, but women continue to remain confined away from each other, divided into or between domestic and public spaces. Surely, *Agnisakshi* does not tell us how we may tear down these walls in the real world. In the story of Devaki and Thankam, Lalithambika only projects her longing into its climactic scene wistfully, giving up realism so that a scene of mutual exchange may shade seamlessly into the image of spaces commingling. That too, perhaps, holds an important message—that it is up to this generation of Malayali women to find ways of dismantling the walls that divide women. As long as Lalithambika's longing continues to echo through our generation in ways distinct to our times, we cannot ignore this task that *Agnisakshi* gestures at, albeit vaguely.

J. Devika

Works Cited

Abdulkhadar, Vakkom M., 1946, *Chitradarshini* (Thrissur: Saraswati Publishing House).

Antharjanam, Lalithambika, 1980, *Agnisakshi* (Thrissur: Current Books).

Kinship Terms

achan Namboodiri	the eldest son of a Namboodiri household; he alone is permitted to marry from the same caste
ammavan	maternal uncle
ammayi	aunt, mother's brother's wife
ammumma	grandmother
aniyan	younger brother
aniyathi	younger sister
aphan Namboodiri	younger Namboodiri, brother to achan Namboodiri; not permitted to marry from the same caste
Bappuji	Hindi for respected father; Gandhiji's followers affectionately called him 'Bappuji'
cheriyamma	younger aunt
edathi	elder sister
ettan	elder brother
kuttan	a pet name, meaning son
kuttikkavu	term used to address a young Namboodiri woman
mataji	respected mother
mol	affectionate way of addressing a young daughter/girl
muthaphan	an elderly uncle, a distant relation

muthassiamma   affectionate way of addressing a grandmother

netyaramma   title given to a Nair woman, wife of a
Thampuran (Kshatriya king) or a Namboodiri

valiamma   elder aunt

AGNISAKSHI

On the Banks of the Ganga

She lay ensnared in the coiled locks of the Lord of Kailasa.[1] Like
a speck, like a dream. Frozen. Hundreds of years passed ... thousands of years ... even yugas ... Then, the voice of an agonized
soul, that of a Rajarshi, beckoned her, 'Please come down. Do
Come. Please redeem my ancestors from their sins. Please give us
life once again.'

The flame of his penance rose up to the mount of Kailasa.
Melting, stirring, overflowing. Following the path that that agonized human soul pointed to, pleading and persuading, she flowed
down. From the heavens to the netherworlds, she fell from the
heights to the depths. And what a fall it was! Shattering and
scattering, foaming and dashing straight ahead. No, she was not
running, she was flowing. A gurgling *galagala*, 'Coming ... I am
coming ... Here I am!'

Water as white as milk, as cool as snow. Sacred water which
washes away all the sins of those who immerse themselves in it.
She stood for a moment gazing at it. Slowly, she took a step down,
one step, then two, her legs grew numb, her teeth chattered. Which
felt cooler, her body or her mind? She remembered: a lifetime's
dream was about to be fulfilled. A feeling of having reached the
place she had always wanted to reach.

[1] One of the peaks of the Himalaya that is believed to be the abode of
Lord Shiva and his consort, Parvathy.

The river called Ganga or Bhagirathi.[2] The sacred river of the epics.[3] The life stream of modernity. Bharatam's very own hallowed river. She was going deeper and deeper into it. The first dip was icy. Freezing cold. And then? An indescribable bliss. A comfort that caressed her soul and body before moving on. A sense of liberation that severed all existing worldly bonds. She felt like a newborn child.

Again and again she dipped in, immersing herself. The waves moved above her head, maybe over her life itself, and disappeared. Were they washing and removing all the dirt, pain, and sorrows endured so far? Was the Mother giving her a rebirth? As she finished her bath, stepped out, and moved through the crowds, why did she feel that someone was holding her hand? Who was that person? A divine presence. In the next bathing ghat, Appu, holding his daughter's hand ... floating the urn containing Ettan's mortal remains in the river. Could that beloved soul have stepped out of that urn and come to her? Telling her, walk slowly, slowly, exactly like he used to when she was young.

The people who came later kept pushing aside those who preceded them. After all, no single person owned the bathing ghat. Here, it was a constant flow. An unending torrent. Moving along with the flow, one is forced to push and pull and walk ahead. Bath over, the religious rituals had to be performed. My children! Where are you?

As the sacred bosom of the Goddess Ganga glowed in the rosy hue of dawn, the water ritual of *aarathi* was performed continu-

---

[2] Another name for the river Ganga. King Bhagiratha through his prayers and penance brought the river Ganga from Mount Kailasa to the earth to give moksha (release) to his ancestors cursed to live in *pathala loka*.

[3] Religious literature, the legendary poetical works of Ramayanam and Mahabharatam.

ously. During the ritual, rice grains, flowers, saffron powder, and a burning wick were placed on a leaf and floated on the river with prayer recitals for an auspicious married life, accompanied by the sound of conch and the chanting of sacred names. Out of the thousands of floating, burning wicks, some might topple almost immediately. Some others would bob along for a long time. Would there be, among them, some that moved and danced through the waves and went a great distance? In any case, this worship of floating burning wicks on the waves continued without a break.

On another day, she too might have bought a leaf, lit a cotton wick, and performed the auspicious aarathi. But today, she had something more precious than that to float here. Today, the flower offerings were the mortal remains of a saintly life. Pure memories. The sorrow and the tears. On the River of Life, how far had this leaf-boat travelled! On many occasions, she had been afraid that she would sink. But she did not. Continuing to flow, she had walked. To sink in this great flow—what did it matter now if it happened?

In the *pitrughat*, the ritualist continued to instruct Devu in the death-ceremony rituals. She took the sesame seeds, flowers, and water in the palms of her hands and offered the *pindam*, the rice-ball offering to the dead. As she watched, her eyes and mind filled. The ritualist recited the mantra. 'Elder brother, Ettan, this is all we have to offer to you. Peace, peace to the fathers, the grandfathers, and the great-grandfathers.' She remembered the generations of people that had gone before her. Father. Mother. Father's father. Mother's mother. Thus, the names of seven generations of people were invoked. All of them, she was the sum total of them all. Probably she was them. She scooped a palmful of Ganga water and performed the water rites for the dead. Let all those who had gone attain moksha. Let those who are yet to come feel fulfilled. An auspicious life to all those who stood before, after, and with her.

'The annual death rites have been performed well.' The ritualist had concluded the rites and blessed the performer. Had they left anything incomplete? Opening a small handheld pouch, she took out a tiny packet, opened it, and raised her hand to throw something into the river. Suddenly she stopped. It was not yet time. There was one more karma, a rite, to be performed. Restless, she looked around anxiously.

The sun had risen higher. The aarathi lamps and the flowers moved and danced on the waves, touched and burnished by the golden sunlight. The Kumbhamela had just concluded. The tirthaghat and the streets around were alive. The town was filled with ochre-robed mendicants. People who had arrived from various places. People who spoke different languages. Naked people. Naga sannyasis. All of them desired moksha, release. What did the word 'moksha' really mean? This bliss which is sought individually. Suddenly from some cave of her past, a sentence reverberated in her mind. 'My penance is for your moksha. I suffer for your pleasure. Please give me at least this pain.'

Who had said that? Who? When? Where? Oh! She had forgotten. Would it be the voice of someone from one of her seven ancestral generations? Or was it the feeble voice of a friend forgotten even while living?

Tired, while climbing the steps she paused remembering something. 'Haven't I heard that she was living somewhere here ... She ... She ... What would her present name be?'

In Hindi, she asked an old sannyasi who stood by her, 'Do you know where Swami Suddhananadaji's ashram is? How far is it from here?'

He turned and looked at her. 'That ... that ... I do not know for sure. It could be in Rishikesh,[4] or in Vyasaguha, or Vasisthaguha.[5]

[4] One of the holy places on the slopes of the Himalayas.
[5] Sacred caves on the slopes of the Himalayas.

I am not from here. Please ask that Mataji sitting over there. She would definitely know.'

A yogini seated on the wide step on the tirthaghat was immersed in meditation. She was surrounded by disciples who sang sacred verses and rang small bells. They were also performing the water rituals with a circling motion of hands. A glowing motherly presence. On seeing her, anyone would feel like bringing their palms together and paying obeisance. When the crowds grew thinner, she fell at the Holy Mother's feet. She felt cool fingers on her forehead.

'Peace. Peace. May you be blessed with peace.'

With uncontrolled anxiety she asked, 'Amme! Do you know where Swami Suddhanandaji's ashram is? Could you please point the way to that place?'

Without raising her head the Holy Mother said, 'Bhagavan Suddhanandaji has attained *nirvanam*.'

'I know that. But there is a relative of mine, a woman who was his disciple. I want to see her.'

A tremor passed through the Holy Mother; she seemed startled. Her forehead quivered. 'Gurudevan had many disciples. How can we know about one such person? What is her name?'

Her name ... name ... What should she say? Devaki Manampalli? Devi Bahen? Tethi Edathi? She stood thinking for a while. 'She is a Brahmin woman of the clan of Sree Sankara.[6] Her name is Devaki. She was called Devi Bahen. She is a close relative of mine. I have been separated from her for a long time. I do not know her present name.'

Mataji looked at her suspiciously and asked, 'What is the name of this relative of Devi Bahen?'

---

[6] Adi Shankara, the most revered Hindu philosopher and theologian who consolidated the doctrine of Advaita Vedanta, monism.

She repeated her old and present names—named Lakshmi, later addressed as Thankam, she was now known as Mrs K.M.K. Nair.

Once again Mataji's countenance paled. Did those unemotional eyes fill? Did her graying eyebrows pucker? Her face mirrored a pain that broke its bonds and lost control.

What a resemblance!

What a resemblance ...

Suddenly, doubt bloomed in Mrs Nair's mind. Clasping Mataji's feet she sobbed and asked, 'Forgive me. Was your previous abode near Choorni River in central Kerala? And your former name ...'

Mataji was intensely disturbed. Even before the question formed itself, she stopped it. 'Enough. Please understand. A *sannyasini* has no past life. No. None at all. She should not either. I am a sannyasini. I am known by the name Sumitrananda. That's all you need to know.'

She rose hastily. She climbed the steps with her disciples, and walked on ahead till she was absorbed in the vast crowds that spread around and disappeared from sight.

As she stood staring, Mrs Nair's eyes filled. Her heart pounded. 'My Devi Bahen. My elder sister ... my ... my guru, teacher ... Have you, after giving us moksha, begun to pursue your own? Is this real moksha? After rejecting all those who are close to you? Then ... then ... you have now failed. On this day we met. We recognized each other. I shall never leave you alone again.'

Twisting the small bundle she held, Mrs Nair stood, stunned and benumbed. It was not quite clear to her whether she had lost or gained a valuable object that she had long searched for and finally found. What had happened was unclear.

Memories of Childhood

'Amme!' It was when her son gripped her shoulders and called her that she woke up. 'Amma, are you going to turn sannyasin and renounce the world? If you felt this detachment after a single dip in the Ganga, what would happen by the time you end your pilgrimage?'

'No, son, don't worry about that,' she had laughed. 'This mother will not renounce life. If she was so inclined, it would have happened a long time ago.' Mrs Nair did not fully express what she felt. Suddenly, struck by a thought she asked, 'My child, do you believe in destiny?'

'No. Isn't that what all of you have jointly taught me? I believe that there is nothing beyond or greater than man. The physical sciences declare so. But, for your sake, Amma, I go through all these artificial rituals.'

'All right.' She sighed deeply. 'Ammavan used to say "Intelligence runs ahead on the path of destiny. Intelligence is what leads the human being." So, there is nothing greater than destiny. Today, that became clear to me. In all my life, there hasn't been a single day like this one, but you won't understand. All right, must we return this very day?'

'Yes, we have to. I have just a day's leave.'

'Forgive me, my son!' the mother pleaded, 'Let's stay here for two more days. For some reason, I just don't feel like leaving this place. Memories of your Ammavan ... about your Ammayi too ... Aha! ... What a fate ... If not fate—how could this come to be?'

She stood exhausted. He raised his face to her. He had never heard his mother talk this way. She had never asked for any concessions. He had never seen her like this before, filled with sorrow and oppressed by her thoughts.

'All right. We'll do as you wish. We can rent a room in a good hotel. Devu is very tired. Isn't she her grandmother's darling daughter? Hold on to her ...'

Leaning on her granddaughter's shoulder she walked along slowly, asking many people, 'Where is the ashram of the Mataji from *yogini madhom*? How far is it from here?'

Many of them were startled. Some said, 'Isn't that in Kasi?[7] Rishikesh? Badrinath?[8] ...' No one could answer precisely. An old mendicant said, 'If you are referring to Sumitranandasaraswathi, her abode is four *katham*s from here, on the banks of the Ganga. She is a learned woman. She accepts only women disciples. If you go at the time of the satsang, late in the evening, anyone can see her.'

Her granddaughter was very tired. Having wandered around the whole day, she must be hungry. She might even be bored. The gap between sixty and sixteen is considerable. Why had she brought this playful girl along with her? Did she, out of respect for the older generations, think that only when water was poured through her young granddaughter's hands, moksha was possible? Or was

---

[7] Kasi or Benares, is an important pilgrimage centre that is famous for its Shiva temple. People believe that a visit to the Kasi temple and a dip in the Ganga that flows by the city will rid them of all their sins and help them to obtain moksha.

[8] Other sacred pilgrimage centres of India.

it on account of a senseless false pride? She held the sleepy child close to her.

They rented two rooms in a big hotel. Tasty food. Comfortable beds. But, for some reason, Mrs Nair did not feel like eating anything. She was silent as she sat at the dining table.

'Mother, if today is a day on which you eat only one meal, shall I ask them to fetch some milk and bananas? If you don't eat anything, you will suffer from acidity later. You will fall ill.'

'No, Kuttan, I don't want anything. Both of you eat and go to bed. Let me sit on this terrace for a while. A nice breeze is blowing. And nice sights as well, being a sacred place.'

He understood that his mother was very disturbed. She was deep in meditation and did not want to talk. She looked as though she was in the grip of a powerful memory. On the open verandah, she stretched out on a canvas chair. The cool breeze from the Ganga was sweeping up. Down below, in the streets, the crowds moved. The sound of conches and the chanting of prayers reverberated in the air. Does this tirthaghat never sleep? All kinds of people, the learned, the detached, the pleasure-loving, and the charlatans quoting the Vedas could be seen among them. If moksha is a truth, how very few would actually attain it!

Suddenly, that old saying came back to her, 'My penance is for your moksha. I feel sorrow for your pleasure. Please give me at least this sorrow.'

No, Edathi, no. This too I shall share. Today onwards, that sorrow is mine too. You who have sacrificed everything for the welfare of all of womanhood, please give me at least this memory ...

Mrs Nair continued to gaze into the distance. The path towards the past stretched right up to the end. A familiar village. A house. No Mrs Nair. No Devi Bahen. No Sumitrananda. Only plain, simple Tethikutty. Tethikuttykkavu. Young mistress. Elder sister. In a sari worn in the traditional way with its narrow gold border;

chittu and *cheruthali* adorning her neck, brass bangles on her wrists; slim, pale bride of Manampalli mana. It was the procession before her installation as a bride of the house. There was drumming and ululation. Nadaswaram too. The sound of Vedic chants. Valiya Ettan, with his gentle expression, tall, fair-skinned, wearing a *thattu* and shoulder cloth, walking in front of her. Behind, surrounded by a jostling crowd of palm-leaf umbrellas, a figure covered by the *mantrakodi*. Hennaed feet moving slowly. She climbed slowly, placing one foot before the other. Once again, the chorus of auspicious blessings; ululations and sounds of celebration.

The Chief Priest (Otikkan Namboodiri) said, 'Pray to your family goddess and offer her your heartfelt salutations. Then enter your new home, right foot first.'

'*Aarappoove ... pooy ... pooy!*'

'*Kalu, kalu ... kalu ... kalu!*'

The sound of ululation, celebration, and festivity.

Women carrying brass plates bearing auspicious objects stood on either side and welcomed them. Red *tecchi* flowers and fried grain were showered on them like rain. An auspicious deity (bride) was being installed at Manampalli mana. The succession to the *tharawad* depended on her.

In the inner courtyard, with drawings of rice flour, where a measure of paddy and the auspicious brass lamp were placed, Ettan and Edathiamma sat on the *aavanappalaka*. Married women circled fistfuls of rice and flowers before placing both over their heads. They were fed sweets. In the rectangular outer verandah, young Namboodiri boys were clamouring to snatch the sweet cakes and fried grain before running away. In order to witness these scenes, a fourteen-year-old girl hastily tried to squeeze herself into the inner verandah. When she reached the end of the inner verandah, she heard a harsh voice, '*Hai, Hai*, move over, child. You have touched everything and polluted them. You will make us all go blind. Just because you are Aphan Namboodiri's daughter, do you cease to be a Sudra woman?'

The girl stood stunned. Whose voice was that? Ettan's mother's? The water-crazed grandmother? Or that of the insane younger aunt? Or was it a combination of all their voices?

The young girl lowered her head and backed away. She flushed, her eyes brimmed with tears, her lips quivered. If those words came from that limping water-crazy grandmother, who muttered constantly, carrying a vessel of water, she did not have to take it seriously. So too if it was that insane younger aunt, whom everyone normally ignored. On a normal day, while everyone watched, she could have made a face and run away. But, today, on this special day, in the presence of so many invited guests, this insult was unbearable. By the time she reached her mother, Netyaramma, who had withdrawn into the corner of the outer verandah, she was sobbing.

Netyaramma was taken aback.

'Thankam! Are you crying? Shame on you! On this happy occasion, why are you crying? Why?'

'I want to see Unni Ettan's Edathiamma. My own Edathiamma. Those Namboodiri women are not letting me into the inner verandah, saying that I am a Sudra woman!' Thankam sobbed.

Netyaramma laughed, 'Foolish girl! Is that why you are crying like this? Let the installation take place. Then we can see her. After today, we can see her every day. Actually, the young bride has been brought in for our viewing, I mean you and me, specifically!'

But the only daughter of the mighty strong-willed Aphan Namboodiri knew no compromise. She would not tolerate insults. Indoors, cheers and happy sounds. Young Namboodiris dashing about and snatching sweet cakes and fried grain. The young bride seated on a woven grass mat on the outer verandah. Thankam was prohibited from entering that space because she was a Sudra woman. Why was she, the daughter of Manampalli Aphan Namboodiri, a Sudra woman? She had no need of any prohibited comfort or pleasure.

Pushing aside her mother's hands, she stepped into the court-yard and ran. She did not cry. She had no complaints against any-one. She stepped into the *pathayappura* of the *mana*, known as Kacheri Malika, entered her parents' room, and closed the door. Pretending that nothing had happened, she tried to read her school books. Netyaramma was well aware of her daughter's obduracy. When she did not respond to the four or five messengers, food was sent in to her. Despite great persuasion, Thankam did not touch even a morsel. She was not hungry and had no appetite either. From outside came the sounds of people returning happily after the installation feast.

Someone said, 'The mistress is not a match for the young mas-ter. She is not that fair-skinned. Just think of the young master's complexion, dignity, and appearance, that look of distinction on his face, what do you say ...'

'Does being fair and pale make you beautiful? This girl has a fresh, healthy glow, thick eyelashes, marked eyebrows. In my opinion, the young mistress has an auspicious appearance,' said another.

Yet another said, 'Look here, no point being bothered by com-plexion, dignity, and so on. This is a matter of matching horo-scopes. I hear that the young master's horoscope has a flaw, the "*chovva dosham*". Do you know how many horoscopes were examined and rejected before Sankara Variar chose this one? She is an excellent match for the young master. Good for the tharawad also. Has there ever been such a feast like this before? Didn't the senior master himself personally serve the *payasam*?'

Lying alone and silent, Thankam heard everything.

A picture formed in her mind—a young woman with the complexion of a tender mango leaf, thick eyelashes, modest demeanour holding the payasam ladle, sweetness, only sweetness, blessed sweetness.

Had she fallen asleep?

Was this a dream?

Edathiamma

It was a famous tharawad. Many members and wealth to match. They maintained an elephant, a howdah, and palanquins—all symbols of their social standing. One of their ancestors had been a *Dewanji*, a representative of the British Raj. Another, a commander of the army. Her grandmother's grandmother's grandmother had been the wife of the Maharaja. From that time, they had been accorded the title of 'Netyaramma'. The men were called 'Patanayars'. Only royalty and wealthy Namboodiris had a *sambandham* with the women of that house. At the time, the tharawad was blazing with glory, and members even had the power to kill and arrange murders.

Caught in the flow of time, everything changed. Wealth dwindled and members increased. Young maidens did penance waiting for partners, for *thampuran*s or *thirumeni*s. Restricted to reciting prayers and offering the first puja of the day in temples, their lives had shrivelled. It was at that time that Manampalli Aphan Namboodiri saw Ammalukutty of Nair veedu and became fascinated by her. Aphan Namboodiri was well into his forties. Ammalu Amma was sweet seventeen. Even so, the Nair veedu family viewed this liaison as good fortune.

Manampalli mana was a famous Namboodiri household of central Kerala. While the naive Achan Namboodiri bathed, prayed, played chess, and spent most of his time in the fore verandah, Aphan Namboodiri ruled the tharawad. The paddy from all the fertile fields of the region poured into the granaries of Manampalli. Majestic elephants were tied at its gates. The rent from the lands, converted into money, multiplied with interest in the safekeeping of moneylenders. It was well known that the mighty, crafty Aphan Namboodiri could do almost anything in the land of Bhoomi Malayalam, meaning those regions where Malayalam was spoken. Nothing was impossible for him.

The women of Nair veedu had never stepped out of their houses. The men seeking liaisons visited their homestead. But when Aphan Namboodiri renovated the two-storied building next to his *illam*, named it 'Kacheri Malika', and installed Ammalu Amma as his wife there, no one objected. He gave his wife the pleasures and comforts unavailable even to the queen of the land. Of the many children that he had had, Thankam was the only surviving one, and he loved her dearly. Even so, she could barely remember the occasions when her father had touched her or carried her. Aphan Namboodiri was a strict practitioner of the customs and habits observed by an orthodox Namboodiri family. His meals were at his illam, his religious rituals at the temple. To manage the affairs of the household, he travelled tirelessly between the courts and along the village paths. Thankam yearned to sleep in the arms of her father and be kissed by him. Netyaramma would say, 'Mol, please don't pollute your father by touching him. He has arthritis and shouldn't be bathing frequently.'

And so, she grew accustomed to that way of being.

But there was one person whom Thankam could always touch and oblige to bathe again and again—Unni Ettan, who visited the Kacheri Malika whenever he was free. He spent as much time as possible there; sleeping or studying because he was never free to do what he really wanted to in the crowded routine of the main house. Besides Thankam, Netyaramma also loved Unni very much. 'Whenever I see Unni Thirumeni, my eyes brim ... I too had a son of the same age. Till the age of seven, I raised them together. Then ...' Pain choked her before she continued. 'Unni, you must view her as your own sister. Thankam has no other elder brother.'

'Nor I, a younger sister!'

That was true. Barely six months after Aniyan Namboodiri was born, their father died. His fever had intensified after the cold dip in the pond at Karkitakam *vavu* before the annual ceremonies for his ancestors. After that, Ettan had grown up under Aphan's strict control and Netyaramma's loving care.

When a tutor was hired to teach Thankam English, her mother had said, 'Let Unni also learn the language. In future, when he goes to the court to manage the family affairs, shouldn't he know the language?'

But Aphan Namboodiri forbade it. 'The Namboodiris of Manampalli Illam have not yet been reduced to learning that barbaric language. Or, if it ever becomes that vital, there is always Aniyan. He will do.'

So, under the tutelage of Sastri Swami, Ettan learnt Sanskrit. Vadhyan Namboodiri taught him the Vedas. He would be up at three in the morning to bathe. After completing the rituals, study, and meal, he would come straight to Kacheri Malika. After that, they would begin their joint studies. Unni Ettan would teach her Sanskrit. She would teach Unni Ettan English. Ettan, who never talked much, sat smiling in front of her as she talked non-stop about this and that. The day he learnt that his wedding was fixed, he came to Kacheri Malika secretly and whispered to her, 'I am bringing a present for you, Thankam. Can you guess what it is?'

'A bangle.'

'No.'

'A chain.'

'Not that either.'

'Then—a fine mundu.'

'No.'

'I admit defeat. Tell me.'

With an impish smile, Ettan said slowly, 'An Edathi of gold ... an Edathi like you ... an Edathiamma ... would you like her, Thankam ...?'

'Why not? Why would I not like her? An Edathi is coming ...' She broke into peals of laughter.

Ettan covered her mouth.

'Shsh ... don't let Aphan hear it.'

It was when such an Ettan had brought that wondeful Edathiamma, that she had come away in a huff without waiting to see her. A burning sensation inside her was fuelled by sorrow and a sense of guilt. Her head smouldered. Lying dejected, she fell asleep.

The next morning she was burning with fever. She faintly recalled hearing Netyaramma wailing that her daughter was delirious.

'What happened to my child, oh, Guruvayoorappan![9] My Thankam is shivering. How she burns. Yesterday, even as she stepped out of the mana and ran, I knew something was wrong.'

Thankam did not know that the apothecary and the sorcerer had attended upon her. She asked the same question again and again, 'Amme, where is Unni Ettan? Where is he? Is Unni Ettan angry with me? Has he gone away? Is Edathiamma also angry?'

Netyaramma explained to her that Unni Thampuran was not angry with her. Custom demanded that he should not leave his illam for four days after his wedding. At the illam, he sat preparing the medicines for Thankam and prescrbing the customary treatment to be observed by Thankam's mother. 'When you get better, we'll go and visit him. Now, please lie quietly and rest.'

[9] Sree Krishna installed as the deity of the famous temple of Guruvayoor, a locality in central Kerala.

She made no fuss about drinking the bitter herbal concoctions or swallowing the pills. After all they were prepared by her Ettan. Her own Ettan. Dear Unni Ettan.

On the day when her fever subsided and she bathed, Nani Amma, the assistant of the illam, reported, 'The beauty of the bride, our young mistress. Her behaviour. Her gentle habits. Her Excellency never speaks much. So what? Those eyes. What a glow in that gaze! Thick eyelashes. Shapely eyebrows. Thankam, you have not seen her. Your bond with the young master. Won't she be wanting to see her young sister? Can she visit you? No. Child, do go over just once.'

But, how could she? She felt hesitant. A certain reluctance. How could she face the grandmother, who washed and rinsed her hands continuously, and the insane younger aunt? How could she manage a sight of Edathiamma? Thankam stepped into the courtyard and stood thinking. The pond in which the *antharjanam*s bathed was situated on the left side of the path to the illam from Kacheri Malika. On the path between the kitchen and the bathing house stood an Asoka tree to which a swing was fastened. Long ago, Thankam's Ettan had arranged it for her. No man ever used that path. Sunk in all kinds of thoughts, she went down the steps very slowly and sat on the swing. Earlier, it was Unni Ettan who used to push the swing for her. Leaping and swinging higher and higher, even after she touched the leafy branches she used to yell, 'Higher! Higher!' It was on one such occasion as she swung down that the seat had struck Ettan's forehead, wounding him and knocking him out. To this day, the scar lingered. She had never used the swing again.

Recalling past events, Thankam forgot herself. Thus it was that she became aware of the young woman who stepped down from the northern room and walked towards the bathing house. She saw the woman only after she had drawn very close to her. She looked at her bemused. The woman returned her look for a look.

A slim young woman with thick eyelashes, curly hair, with the colouring of tender mango leaves. Possibly two years older than herself. Was she prettier? They stood gazing at each other, as if searching for something.

That young woman spoke familiarly to Thankam, 'I heard that you like the Durga Puja offerings, rice cake, and pounded grain. As I was going to the pond, I saw you sitting here. So, I returned to fetch them for you ...'

She did not ask whether she was Thankam. She did not even enquire whether she was Aphan's daughter. She extended the banana leaf bundle to Thankam as if by long practice. Without contact, Thankam cupped her palms and received that offering. Did she bring her palms together in obeisance? Did her eyes fill? This goddess had blessed her the moment she appeared before her. A sob broke from her.

'Edathi! ... I have only one Edathi.'

'I know. I was waiting for you, Thankam. Why didn't you come to me?'

Thankam narrated the story of her illness. She talked about Ettan. She described the grandmother obsessed with water and the insane younger aunt. Edathi stood listening to everything and finally said, 'Thankam, come to the illam whenever you are free. With no one to keep me company, I am somewhat ...' She continued after some thought, 'When I was in my own illam, I had my elder brother for everything—to play, learn, and read. Thankam, you do not know my elder brother. If not for him, where would I be?'

In a mocking tone, Thankam said, 'Here too there is an Ettan to keep you company.' Pausing, she continued with a soft smile,

'How is Unni Ettan, Edathi? Poor thing! He is always involved in prayers and rituals. He has not so much as looked at a woman or talked to her. My mother used to say, I think that young Master Unni will turn out to be some sort of a renunciate.'

'What is the guarantee that he won't yet?' Edathi said calmly, 'He married only to keep the family going. It was done strictly to maintain the state of a householder. For the rituals, you need a wife. My elder brother used to always say, one who is not good enough for this world, will not be good enough for the next one either. But here, I think everything is done for the sake of the next world.'

Thankam saw the corners of her thick eyelashes moistening. Did her voice turn hoarse? She was a bride. Even so ... Why this? Though Thankam was a naive young girl who had no knowledge of the world, she said, 'Edathi, you will never see another gem like Unni Ettan. Please love my Ettan well.'

Suddenly, Edathiamma gripped her neck and shoulders in an embrace and sobbed. The brass bangles clattered. The small thali shone.

'I am afraid, Thankam. Do I qualify to be the wife of such a great man from such a well-known illam? Am I that fortunate? May the Lord protect me.'

The mid-noon sunlight grew cooler. There was the sound of fire-crackers from the temple. The water-obsessed grandmother held her clothes in a bundle and went towards the pond. Tethi Edathi said anxiously, 'It is very late. There is a great deal of work in the kitchen. I must take a bath and then do the rituals ... Thankam, do come tomorrow also. I haven't had enough of you.'

In the Darkness of the *Nalukettu*

At her age, Thankam had no idea that in order to gain something you might have to endure some great loss. She gained Edathiamma's love, but time spent with Ettan began to diminish. After his wedding, Ettan's responsibilities increased. Early in the morning, there were rituals—*oupasanam* and *vaisyam*. Besides, Aphan Namboodiri began to involve Unni more and more in household matters, saying, 'Won't he one day shoulder the responsibilities of the entire family? He should not be ignorant about family issues. Let him learn a few things about the illam.' Young master Unni did not have time even for his everyday reading. What then of casual talk with his womenfolk?

Thankam too had a great deal to study in school. Even so, she made it a point to spend time at the mana. Not seeing her Edathiamma at least once a day was unbearable. How soon she had learnt to love Tethi Edathi! Even as she loved her, Thankam felt a deep sympathy for Tethi Edathi. She, Tethi Edathi, was not meant for this family. She was not the right wife for the gentle, patient Unni Ettan in this Manampalli mana—ruled by the obstinate and rough Iraviravi Namboodirippad; or this *anthapuram* controlled by women who stuck rigidly to archaic customs—such as the older and the younger aunt or the water-crazy grandmother. This Edathi was not meant to be born into this accursed society. Just recalling it made her eyes brim with tears. How much Edathi had suffered! Poor woman! All kinds of sorrows! The sense of bearing the sorrows of the whole world, where had she got it from?

In the western upper storey bedroom—once Achan Namboodiri's, then Unni Ettan's mother's, and now Unni Ettan's—a mattress had been spread on the wooden cot, hung from the rafters. Incense burned. The bookshelf, placed against the wall, was stacked with thick books in Sanskrit. Below that, on a wooden box, modern novels and books of poetry lay piled up. Tethi Edathi's huge box was not filled with clothes. There was a general complaint that it held only bits of paper. At the sound of her footsteps, Edathi would begin to ascend the stairs. That was an invitation. Following her, Thankam too would go up the stairs. Then, both of them sat down together and would begin to talk or read.

By day, Unni Ettan never set foot in this room. Even at night, he visited it only after consulting the almanac: the tradition of Manampalli mana. Ettan's mother was very particular about such things. Achan Namboodirippad, her husband, had not only married twice in his own community, but had had liaisons at the palace and with the women of the Variar community. He searched for auspicious days to enter his bedroom. And hadn't she, his wife, conceived and delivered several times? She seemed to believe that a union between man and wife was unacceptable if its aim was not to produce children. In her opinion, Namboodiri women were to restrict their entire lives to the kitchen and the prayer room. Their destiny was to read only the Ramayanam and the *Shiva Puranam*.[10] She often said words to this effect in Tethi Edathi's hearing, as though she was hinting at something.

Edathi often said mournfully, 'I never thought it would be this bad, Thankam. When the wedding was being discussed, my elder brother said, "Manampalli Illam is wealthy and powerful. Unni is young ... this is his first marriage ... still I feel an uneasiness

10 A sacred poem on Lord Shiva.

... in the darkness of that antiquated *nalukettu*, how will Tethi survive ...'"

'My mother and uncle consoled themselves saying that everything would work out well with the passing of the present generation. The horoscopes match very well. The dowry terms are agreeable. A famous tharawad! Besides, where can one find a perfect bridegroom.'

With great pain, Edathi would continue, 'Thankam, I am not unhappy that Ettan is unable to be with me all the time. I am not even sorrowful about the disdain shown by the women of the illam. If only I could get something interesting to read! In my illam, we used to get newspapers and magazines. How many books in the almirah! My elder brother would pass on everything he read. He would also explain anything I did not understand. But, within these four walls, I have no books other than the Ramayanam and the story of Seelavathy.[11] When I mentioned this to Ettan, he remarked, "That's good, isn't it?" I don't think Ettan loves anyone. He is afraid of everything and everyone. Aphan, mother, traditions—why, God himself! Like my elder brother said, if I continue to live here, I too might go mad with fear.'

Many newspapers and magazines were being delivered at Kacheri Malika. Father never read them. Nor Ettan. But, Netyaramma needed something to while away her time. Thankam promised that after her mother had read them, she would bring these magazines and papers to Edathi. Aphan Namboodiri had been reluctant to have Thankam learn English; reluctant too about her being educated in modern ways. But, Netyaramma had insisted. In the days to come, Namboodiri or thampuran bridegrooms might not be available for their daughter. If they wanted a good bridegroom,

---

[11] A legendary heroine, noted for her loyalty to her leper husband, who through her penance and virtue prevented the sun from rising to save her husband from death.

she should be suitably educated. How unattractive the Panikkar veedu[12] girl had been. But she had cleared the tenth standard examination. That was why a sub-judge had garlanded her as his bride. In any case, learning wasn't a sin, was it?

Thus, on her mother's insistence, she began to go to school. She read books. She began to think for herself. She was able to spot how Tethi Edathi's eyes, once wide open and shining, were now gradually sinking into darkness.

As she climbed the stairs, carrying folded newspapers, Ettan's mother scowled. The water-crazy grandmother muttered. The insane younger aunt hawked and spat.

'Isn't she the pet daughter of Aphan Namboodiri ... the Nair veedu offspring ... well ... we too have an antharjanam! Barbarian! Phoo!'

She felt not the slightest discomfort at these scolding abuses. Just recently, when she met Ettan she had said, 'Unni Ettan! I'll give you a book. Will you read it? After reading it, please read it out to Edathi also.'

'What book is that, Thankam, do give it to me.'

'A recent novel, a good one. I mean a story book. It is written by a high-class Namboodiri, who studied both Vedas and Vedanta— like you. Want to hear the name of the book? *Aphan's Daughter.*'[13]

Unni Ettan laughed. 'I don't need a book for that, Thankam. Especially when you stand before me.'

She too had laughed.

'But, Ettan, some people can't understand anything, even if they come face to face with it. Nor even if they hear it described. They

[12] The name of a joint family Nair household (tharawad) in Kerala.

[13] Considered a milestone work, this novella was written during the 1930s by a Namboodiri, Mudringot Bhavatratan, during the Namboodiri social reform movement.

have to experience it. This is the story of people who have actually experienced things. Check with Edathi? ...'

Even though the words were from a fifteen-year-old girl, Ettan must have understood that the idea was someone else's. After some time, he said apologetically, 'I know that your Edathi is a very knowledgeable person. I too like conversing with her. But if I spend all my time in the women's quarters, what would people say? Shouldn't there be some decorum in these matters?'

'Ettan, let those who are talking, talk. Why should we bother? How are we affected by that? Such a wonderful Edathi we've got. Both of you love each other. So you should talk freely to each other. After all, you are her Namboodiri husband. And, isn't she your wife and companion? Is it anyone else's business?'

'Maybe not. But ...' Ettan continued hesitantly, 'But, will it do if we consider only our likes and dislikes? Mustn't we pay some attention to other people's wishes? Doing things in the manner suggested by you is not Manampalli Illam's tradition. In this illam, the purpose of married life is not pleasure, but dharma. Child, life is a great *yagnam*. A fire yagnam. Ultimately, Edathi too will understand this.'

Oh! Words heard all those years ago! Had they been prophetic? Would they come true? When she thought of it, she trembled. On that day, what she had felt was anger. These Namboodiris and their preoccupation with dharma! All applicable only to their Namboodiri wives. Then, saying that the almanac did not permit them to enter the bedroom, they forsook their wives and roamed around like temple stud bulls—she had wanted to quote all this, which she had read sometime, somewhere. But, all she said was, 'Poor thing, my Edathi! Poor soul!'

In the Shadow of the Past

Time rolled backwards. Figures and sounds became clearer. They did not feel like memories at all. It all seemed so alive. Hardly a year after Tethi Edathi's wedding, the disturbed younger aunt passed away. She was very old and senile, and had died after a long illness. As the popular expression went, it could be said that she had left this world or attained moksha. She was their granduncle's wife and had died childless, so it was unnecessary to observe the customary year-long *deeksha*. However, Unni decided to observe the ritual. Every day, he performed the death ceremonies for his aunt. A year of complete celibacy. Aphan Namboodiri said nothing, but Netyaramma intervened. 'You don't need to, dear Unni! You've only just got married. She was neither your mother nor father. Not even your own grandmother. All you need to do is to offer the pindam. If you are very particular, observe the rituals for forty-one days. That will do.'

'According to the *sastra*s, that will do. But I believe in a Truth of my own, Thankam's Mother! I had given my word to her at the age of ten. Should I not fulfil it? She got nothing from life. At least in death let her receive some respect through our rituals and observances.'

Thankam remembered all the old stories that she had heard. The insane younger aunt had not always been insane. When she first came to the tharawad, she had been beautiful. Eighteen years old, rosy-complexioned, large-eyed, and full-breasted, she had a very slight limp. Later, Muthaphan had thrown something at her and smashed an eye. Afterwards, he had tugged and torn her earlobes. Theirs had been an 'exchange marriage'.[14] An ageing Muthaphan had married her in order to facilitate Unni's aunt's marriage. But he already had another wife and children who were older than his bride. Muthaphan's other 'wife', Madhavi Varasyar's prowess and influence were famous. She ruled her husband. Muthaphan spent his nights at her house and the day at the pathayappura of the mana, arriving at his illam only to eat. Even while offering water ritually for the wife at mealtimes, he would not raise his head to look at her. The mad younger aunt wept and wept. After that, she took to muttering. In the end, she turned violent. At night, she would stand guard at Madhavi Varasyar's gatehouse. 'I too am going to sleep here. After all, this is where my Namboodiri is.' Madhavi Varasyar would scold her. The younger aunt would curse, 'May you contract smallpox! Let your children's heads be smashed! Oh, Lord of Chengamanad[15] temple, Shiva! This woman stole my husband!'

'You ... you ... stupid woman! I will kill you!' When Muthaphan ran behind her yelling and trying to beat her, she too would roar and run dragging her lame leg. If he caught her, he would slap her about. For her, even a thrashing was pleasurable: Muthaphan touched her at least to beat her. After such aggressive encounters, both would fall ill. Thereafter, for a while, there was peace.

Netyaramma would say, 'That poor elderly antharjanam! Is it her fault that she went mad? If you do not get your wedded Namboodiri to spend at least one night with you, who will not go mad? But that Thirumeni also suffered quite a lot. After installing

---

[14] The custom of two brothers from two different families marrying each other's sisters.

[15] A village close to Alwaye in central Kerala.

her as his wife, he did not have a single night's rest. If someone yells "*pooppupuvey*" and runs around the house, who can sleep?'

Once, when Unni was small and heard all this scolding and beating, he felt very sorry, and gripping Muthaphan's hands said, 'Enough, Muthaphan, enough. Beat me instead. Please leave poor Cheriyamma alone.'

From that day forth, Cheriyamma grew very fond of Unni. 'Unni, you must offer the pindam rice for me! You must observe deeksha. I have no Unni,'[16] she would say, and make him promise. Probably that was why Unni felt bound to observe deeksha for her. Still, what about his poor young wife! Such a short while after their wedding. She has not even conceived.

'No wonder Cheriyamma went mad. If things go on like this, I too will go mad,' said Edathiamma.

Pausing, she said, 'If you do not go mad, becoming an outcaste will be an alternative—won't it?'

At that time, Thankam had not understood what a husband meant to a wife. So she took these stray comments from Edathi to mean signs of dissatisfaction. Edathi was very fond of young children. To her, their caste did not matter. The young grandson of Nani Amma, the maidservant, used to accompany his grandmother. Pale and thin, a lifeless scrap of a boy, his body was full of scabs and sores. The children made fun of him calling him 'Unnaman'. But Edathi would pet him tenderly. She gave him payasam and *ada*. Using oil, soap, and scrubber, she would make him look good. Once, Unni Ettan's mother scolded her for this pollution. But that did not stop her fondness for the boy. Spending her own money, she bought him books and a slate, and sent him to school. 'Poor boy, Isn't it because he doesn't have money? Imagine if he was a boy from the illam. How well we would have taken care of him!'

---

[16] Unni is an affectionate term meaning 'son'.

Thankam also remembered that that boy had been the only one who wept when Edathi left home.

After many days, a retired army man had come to her flat in Delhi.

'Aren't you Mrs Nair?'

'Yes.'

'The daughter from Manampalli mana ... from Nair veedu ...?'

'Yes. Why?'

'I am Meledath[17] Padmanabhan Nair. Nani Amma's grandson. You used to call me "Unnaman".'

She looked at him, astonished. Could it be true? Was this strapping man that famished withered boy?

'I studied up to the seventh standard and left the village. I got a job in a hotel. After that I joined the army, gradually rising with promotions to the rank of *subedar*. I am now retired and am doing some business here. Recently when I went home to the village, I was told that you are here. Could you please do me a favour? Could you please give me the young mistress's address? She is the one who made me a man. I would like to fall at her feet and weep.'

She stood there feeling guilty. She had not made any effort to search for Tethi Edathi, now Devaki Manampalli. She had not searched for her address. She had not even bothered to think about this Edathiamma, who had once been her soulmate and friend. It had taken this servant, this outsider, to remind her! What could she say?

'Padmanabhan Nair, please make enquiries and keep me informed. I once heard that she was in Wardha.[18] Then I heard she was in Bengal. It seems that for a long time she was in Delhi too. I wonder where she is now.'

---

[17] A Nair tharawad.

[18] A town in Gujarat on the banks of river Sabarmathi where Gandhiji built an ashram.

He sighed, and touched his own chest.

'Here, she is here. In my chest—in my mind. Young mistress's form is imprinted in my life's breath. Amme! I shall look at that and pay my obeisance to her.'

She too unconsciously touched her chest. Was that form in her bosom too?

All these events had taken place many years after she had left the mana. Why had she thought of them now? At that time, she did not know anything about Tethi Edathi. Compared to ordinary antharjanams, how lucky she was! She had come as a bride to a well-known household such as Manampalli. She had a handsome, good-natured, and young husband. They loved each other. Then why was she sad? She was like a caged civet cat. She walked restlessly in the kitchen section, prayer room, and the grounds in front of the bathing house. If Ettan's mother asked her to do something, she would obey. After that, she would go upstairs and begin to read and grow thoughtful. One day, when Thankam was going to school, she waved to her, calling out to her and asking in a secretive way, 'Thankam, if I trusted you to do something, could you do it without anyone knowing? No one in this universe should know of it.'

'Even without Ettan's knowledge?' She had retorted mockingly.

'Yes. Even Ettan should not know about it. Ettan will not like all this. He might even be afraid ...' Edathi lowered her voice anxiously. 'I will give you a letter. Please post it. The reply will come to you, Thankam. You should collect it secretly and bring it to me.'

She was stunned. An antharjanam sending a letter secretly! And the reply also to be kept a secret! She, an accomplice to it! 'Hai! Is this the kind of woman Tethi Edathi was? Was she calling this woman Edathi?'

Edathiamma was panting when she took out a weighty enve-
lope from the folds of her cloth and extended it to Thankam. Her
naked breasts heaved with her sighs. She looked suicidal, as if she
were about to leap into the roaring sea.

She seemed to be saying silently, 'I tried to forgive, Thankam. I
even endured. I am unable to control this feeling. If I continue like
this, I too will go insane like our mad Cheriyamma.'

She wrenched her eyes from Edathi's face and bent to look at
the address written on the letter. The well-formed writing shone.

P.K.P. Namboodiri
... Illam
... Place

Havoo! The letter was addressed to Edathi's elder brother. She
had heard a great deal about him, and not only from Edathi. Wasn't
the name, P.K.P. Namboodiri, mentioned in the headlines of every
significant contemporary event? A good writer. A forceful speaker.
A fearless social reformer, famous in Kerala. In his speeches, he
said that antharjanams did not need the *marakkuda* umbrella 'to
hide behind'. Namboodiris had no need to wear the sacred thread
either. Nor was the practice of rituals connected with pollution
important. The rule of the Emperor should end. The traditional
people considered P.K.P. an outcaste from the community.
Everyone, from Muthassiamma to Aphan Namboodiri said, 'What
a pity! We have installed the sister of this man as the bride of our
illam, this man who moves around, sharing meals with outcastes,
a man who has broken his sacred thread, and is the companion of
Pulayas and Muslims!'

'We can tolerate him disrespecting society. But if you oppose
the government! He will be jailed, nothing less. He who returns
from jail automatically loses caste. Thereafter, no friends, no family. Let that worthless fellow think about it!'

Even the previous day, Thankam had heard Aphan Namboodiri speaking in a warning tone. Visiting antharjanams reported to Thankam, 'That Puthusseri Kuttan! From the platform around the banyan tree at Guruvayoor, he declared that Namboodiri women do not need any umbrellas or companions. It seems they should wear saris and blouses. I just covered my ears and left the place.'

The water-crazy grandmother placed her hands on her head and cursed, 'Shiva! Shiva! Shiva! Shiva! The good deeds of the tharawad are destroyed. Is there no difference between purity and pollution? Oh, Chengannattappa! Please break the heads of these creatures.'

Not a single day passed without Edathi weeping at the curses rained on her elder brother. Everyone looked at her meaningfully, saying sarcastic and hurtful things. Some people started a rumour that they had heard that Tethi had worn a sari and blouse, and admired herself when she visited her illam. They broke open Edathiamma's box and examined its contents. They tore Tethi Edathi's books and papers and flung harsh words at Thankam who provided her with them.

Was it possible that Unni Ettan was unaware of these happenings? Or, was he silent because of his gentle nature? Unni Ettan had always been like this. He could not bear to oppose anyone. He believed in all the traditional customs, a man who entered his own wedded wife's chamber only on auspicious nights. One day she asked, 'Ettan, do your Vedas and Puranas say that you should give up your wife? That you should not look at her? In that case, why did you marry her?'

Ettan replied unemotionally, 'Child, I will never give her up. She knows this. But neither will I give up Amma, my family, or the values of my clan. I will not abandon respect for gurus and elders. You should not ask that of me, Thankam.'

She knew that Edathi was changing slowly. Inside that slim body, a volcano smoked and burned. The sob of a lonely heart yearning for change. Sometimes, in despairing disillusionment, it might turn into protest. At other times, it was only a sigh. How many things had they talked about standing beneath the mango tree, in the bathing house, or in the darkness of the *machu*. Reading about her elder brother's speeches and deeds in the newspapers, she would say enviously, 'Thankam, I often think if only I had been a man. If I were a man, I would free not only my wife but all women. I would have given my life for the freedom of the country and for humanity.'

When she gazed at her Edathiamma's glowing face worshipfully, she would think, 'She is growing. Growing inwardly, she is rising. Had she not been an antharjanam, she would have attained a greater status than P.K.P. or Unni Ettan.'

It was that Edathi, weeping and uneasy, who now handed her a letter. 'This message has to reach its destination.' 'I shall get it across, Edathi. For good or bad, I will support you. But, my ... my ... destiny ... please do not ensnare it in this! Please release me! ... You should not make me that cruel woman who demolished her father's tharawad! ...'

Suddenly, somewhere, there towered a burst of ritualistic fireworks. Mrs Nair was startled. Shivering in the early morning breeze, she looked at the Ganga. The waves rippled. There was no end to the flow. Caught in the strong current, not only banana leaves, but trees, timber, and even corpses kept flowing on and on.

It was only then that she realized that it was late, and that she had been sitting in the same position for a long time.

Exchange of Letters

Mrs Nair got up rubbing and stretching her hands and feet frozen by the cold. Her son and his daughter were sleeping peacefully in the next room. Why can't I sleep like that? Was sleeplessness the severest curse of old age? Would she never get a release from this?

Holding on to the half-wall of the terrace, she stood looking into the distance. Over the snow-clad Chandi Mountain, a single star shone. What radiance! Single stars do shine on the earth, spreading their glow all around, but they were solitary. Was her Edathi one among them? Perhaps Ettan and P.K.P. were also such solitary beings. From behind the veil of forgetfulness, sounds, forms, and experiences were rising and coming alive. Even now, she could hear the tone of the reply Edathi received to her first letter:

I know your sorrows, younger sister. They are not yours alone but of all society. Bear it. When you grow mature through suffering, the time for release will come. Prepare for that day. Unni is a good man. Love him. Try to gain his confidence.

Edathi wrote in reply:

I am trying to bear it, elder brother! I bathe early in the morning. I perform all the religious rituals. I work in the kitchen. I fast. I never argue or answer sharply; not even with the water-crazy muthassi. But my insides are burning and melting. Not a word to read, not a single person to talk to, a life like death ... He does not understand anything, elder brother. He is a divine being, not human. You, who taught me the story of man, why did you get me married to a divine being? Will we ever get along? I read your speeches and your articles. Thankam brings them to me. If not for her, I would have committed suicide a long while back.

It was thus, when she became a permanent character in those letters, that Thankam slipped in a little note without Edathi's knowledge, and posted it along with Edathi's letter. It said:

Forgive me, Blessed one! Thankam is only an address. She is an Aphan's daughter. From another community. It is fashionable for people like you to speak dismissively of people from communities other than yours. Therefore, forgive me. It is enough if you do not hate me.

Her note was prompted by the tragedy of the heroine of the novel *Aphan's Daughter.* The answer to that question arrived in a piece of paper placed along with his reply to Edathi:

Dear unknown maiden! Sulochana was an ideal. But Thankam is a reality. We are not people who sacrifice realities. I am one who believes that a society which does not accept Aphan's daughters has no after life. That is why I am a destroyer of casteism.

On transparent blue paper, in small letters, a note like a star. How many times did she read it? Was it the beginning of something? If she was asked whether she loved P.K.P. Namboodiri, Thankam Nair had no clear answer even today. But she had worshipped him wholeheartedly. She had valued him greatly. Apart from being her dear Edathi's beloved elder brother, hadn't she felt an indescribable affinity with him? She was keener than her Edathi to send letters and receive replies. She recalled that not a single word about romantic love had been exchanged. Nothing that could not be revealed. Still, why had she been so careful not to show Edathi those letters? ... Why had she felt thrilled to read them? Why had she felt so blissful reading those few lines, with only the stars of the sky and the flowers of the earth as witnesses? This aged woman, Mrs Nair, knew that the fleeting emotion people call romantic love was a harmless indulgence. At a certain age, in the hearts of some men and women, this bud shoots up and blossoms, making their lives worth living. They never consider the consequences ... But, it spreads a fragrance during their whole lifetime and lingers like unfading flowers. A woman who has not loved even once, a man who has not loved even once, how unlucky they were!

When those fine sheets of paper were blown like bits of white clouds, Mrs Nair felt thrilled. She remembered that not once had they written anything about themselves. Edathi was the chief topic. He wrote:

Thankam, Please tell your Unni Ettan that a woman is not just an idol or a wooden doll. She needs someone to hold on to ... to climb, to grow. She needs a man to love. In this birth, only Unni can be these two for her.

On another occasion, he wrote:

Console Tethikutty. I have erred by providing her with such knowledge and ideas of freedom. If it was anyone else, I would have advised her to break out, give up everything and come away. But Thankam! She is your sister—the wife of your Unni Ettan. I know that she loves Unni. Please tell Tethi that a relationship once broken would be very difficult to mend.

Even now, the lines which he, an eccentric whom she had not met even once, wrote for the last time, resounded in her ears:

Thankam, I have never addressed you as 'dear'. But, you are very dear to me. My beloved sister's companion. You are intelligent, you are capable of remembering what is worth remembering and forget-

ting what should be forgotten. We have not met. But I like you even though we haven't met ... Romantic love is not something I am destined for. This exchange of letters ends today. Tomorrow, I join the satyagraha movement. I might be beaten to death. I might be imprisoned. Or hanged. In any case, I am lost to the external world. Do not mention this to Edathi. I entrust her to you. You alone!

Even so, Thirumeni, was I able to protect her? Or save her. No one can be another's guardian. When the news broke that P.K.P. Namboodiri was arrested for breaking the law, and Edathi sobbed bitterly, I took a conscious decision not to try and console her. Father scolded her ...'Remember, Tethi, the illam of your birth no longer exists. If you so much as step in there, you cannot return here again.'

Grandmother nagged, 'Shiva Shiva! Shiva Shiva! Our young Namboodiri men seem to be an unprincipled lot. Touching anything and everything, eating anything, no sense of purity, they will go blind and now has the time come for them to land in jail? My Chengannattu Thevar! Shatter his head.'

Valiamma placed a finger on her nose, 'I am just thinking of that mother of Puthusseri. It was after much prayer and offerings that this Kuttan was born to her—a much longed-for child. And look what he's become. The tharawad is ruined. Still the poor thing is bearing it all! ...'

Ettan alone had said nothing, but stood in the prayer room twisting and lengthening the cotton wick in the lamp. In the mana, crowds had gathered expecting a *smarthavicharam*. In a corner of the restroom, Edathi lay face down, sobbing, consoled only by Netyaramma, 'Kuttikkavu, stop crying. After all, what has happened! Your elder brother set out to achieve something good. How many people do that and return after remedial purifications. When that happens, these very people who talk so much will welcome him back.'

Thankam remembered that these words were from the ideas she had given her mother. Amma had no idea about the long exchange of letters between her and P.K.P. On days when P.K.P.'s letters arrived, she used to present the topics discussed in those letters in some other form, turning them into points of general debate. So, Amma would have received an advance announcement of the political and social changes about to take place. She once told Ettan, 'Unnikuttan, buy a sari and a blouse for your young wife. How beautiful she would look in them! ...'

But, no one bought anything for the young mistress. The great unrest that followed P.K.P.'s imprisonment died down. At the mana, bathing, paying obeisance, and religious rituals continued as usual. In the kitchen, huge vessels of rice and vegetables were prepared on time. Aphan Namboodiri went around as usual, involving himself in family matters and lawsuits. Everthing went on as usual. The new flame that blazed in Edathi's tear-stained eyes alone went unnoticed.

She remembered that she had been in the tenth class at that time, and her attention had shifted from P.K.P. and Edathi. Besides politics and romance, how many other things were discussed in her books! She wanted to study, wanted to pass with a first class and to continue studying. She had wanted to pass the BA and the MA examinations. After that, get a job and be independent. Thankam felt that a woman had to be independent and self-sufficient. It was the lack of it that made people like Ettan and Edathi suffer so much. Even before P.K.P. wrote so, she had written that the country's freedom ranked only second to an individual's freedom. She did not know what Aphan Namboodiri thought of educating her ... But Netyaramma would say ... all kinds of things such as 'All she has to do is pass her tenth standard. Trippunithura Tamburan[19]

[19] A prince from the royal house of Cochin whose traditional household was located in the town of Trippunithura.

had requested for her hand in marriage ... So, has Mooppil Nair ...'[20]

Thankam would laugh, 'Even if Poornathrayeesa (Sree Krishna installed at the Thrippunithara temple) or Lord Padmanabha objects, this girl will study till she passes her MA examinations. She will not rest till she has.'

[20] Head of a Nair household.

Will We Meet Again?

Destiny, destiny—does anyone really know what it is all about? Is it a force man can create and control at will? Or, is it like this great flow of the Ganga, a stupendous torrent which shatters everything that tries to merge with it? Be that as it may, she, Thankam, Manampalli Aphan Namboodirippad's daughter and the progeny of Nair veedu, did not believe in destiny at that time. She was prepared to fight any kind of fight to win what she wanted. Life was a battle. For all of them: for herself, P.K.P. Namboodiri, and Edathi who did not know how to wrest what she wanted from life. She was a defeated heroine. And herself? Hadn't she struggled, hadn't she too fought? Even so, how had the story ended? Mrs Nair thought: her parents had decided that she would marry after her tenth-class examination. And she had fared well. Success was certain. Messengers from thampurans and Namboodiris streamed in. Of them, an alliance was almost formed ... The groom was the son of a matriarch, of a well-known *kovilakam*. Good looking! Young! Wealthy! Netyaramma was very happy.

'On the very day she was born, the astrologer, Sankara Variar predicted that as Thankam grew, so too would the tharawad flourish and become a palace. Her horoscope matched that of the ammumma, who had died at Thrippunithara. The good fortune of the tharawad. Our good fortune. O Vadakkunnathan![21] O Guruvayoorappa! Please make this happen!'

[21] Lord Shiva, the deity of the famous temple in Trichur.

'What fortune, Amme. Do tell me about my luck!' Thankam had laughed and asked.

Netyaramma began to repeat the desirable qualities of the bridegroom, 'Thampuran is third in line to head the family; and when that happens, Nair veedu will be safe. Thankam, never forget. Remember this. It has always been the women who improved the fortunes of the tharawad. My great-grandmother's husband presented her with an elephant as his traditional gift on Vishu day. My elder sister retrieved the northern fields from tenants. As for you, you may bring the family a car and extended hillside properties!'

Recalling P.K.P. Namboodiri's words, the sixteen-year old Thankam said, 'Amme, I too will improve our tharawad. But, it won't be through alms from Namboodiris or thampurans. I will study. Study more and come through successfully. And then, I will get an honourable job and improve the lot of the family. Do tell Father that before I achieve this, I will not marry. Chengannattappan is my witness.'

Even now in her mind's eye, she could see Netyaramma's startled face. If she had not held her mother, Netyaramma would have fainted. Had the heavens collapsed, she would not have been this upset. The whole atmosphere at home changed. Aphan Namboodiri, who had been arranging the central wooden pillar of the wedding pandal, entered and heard the news. No one had ever seen her father in such a rage. His burning gaze, as it swept over Thankam from head to toe, might have singed her, '*Um!*' an angry grunt, 'You want to study, do you? I will teach you. Know that Manampalli Iraviravi Namboodiri knows not only how to raise children, but to keep them in their place. You don't want to marry, is it? You ... you ... I will ... I will ...'

'*Tte!*' A forceful blow fell on her left cheek. A blow from a father who had not even pinched her! Even on this distant day, the memory of that blow brought such pain that Mrs Nair stroked her cheek. Did that hurt still linger? That blister? He had dragged his daughter writhing in severe pain and pushed her into a room and locked the door. She heard his order, 'Not even a drop of water for her. Let her study. Let her stay by herself and learn a lesson.'

For Thankam, it was no punishment. She felt no hunger or thirst. Her mind was going through a kind of madness spurred by her mother's sadness, father's anger, and her own unyielding stand. She was disoriented and could not distinguish between night and day. Netyaramma sobbed aloud invoking Vadakkunathan and Guruvayoorappan, and wandered up and down. Father scolded the assistants of Kacheri Malika and verbally attacked the tenants. The servants pressed their empty stomachs, sighed, and muttered. Only later did she learn that during those days no rice had been cooked and that her father and mother had not eaten. How many days went by! One ... two ... or three? ...

In the end, she had woken to Unni Ettan calling her name. He had come after his special rituals at the Chengannat temple, his forehead marked with holy ash, carrying the special temple prasadam, the sweet *thrimadhuram*. 'Thankam!'

She raised her head. Her eyes were full and her heart was heavy.

'Thankam, you used to say that you love your Unni Ettan best, and that you would do anything for him! Is that true?'

'Yes, Etta, I will do anything for you.' She said helplessly. 'Likewise, won't you for me?'

'Any doubt about that Thankam? I say this for your sake, Thankam. Please get up. Eat this payasam. It is the offering to Chengannattappan. Thankam, have you any idea how sad we all are? If you do not want to marry right now, that is all right ... You want to study? ... We'll let you study. I will tell Aphan everything and make arrangements. Come now ... Come and eat something.'

'Unni Etta! You have promised me ... haven't you? Don't go back on it, will you?' That stubborn girl asked hesitantly, 'I want to study. Will you arrange that, Etta?'

'Yes, I will,' Ettan said emphatically.

'Next week, Aniyan will be here. That fellow also wants to study. I will tell Aphan. You can both go together to college. We'll make all the necessary arrangements for you. We'll make it all possible.'

Unni Ettan's younger brother, Aniyettan, had from infancy stayed at his maternal grandmother's home, the beloved child of the family. She had heard from one source that Aniyan's progressive maternal uncle had sent him to school. But Aphan Namboodiri pretended ignorance of this arrangement. As far as he was concerned, Unni was the most important person. Unni would maintain and uphold the tradition of Manampalli Illam. Also, it might have crossed his mind that if Aniyan learnt something of the barbarian language, it would come in handy in dealing with legal matters.

Since it all happened at the time Thankam offered peaceful resistance in battle mode, no one questioned Aniyan's higher education. After all, he was the younger son and had to make his way in the world not being eligible to head the household. And Netyaramma was secretly pleased that he would be a support and companion to her daughter.

From Chengannattu village, one had to walk for three miles or cover the same distance by bullock cart, then cross the river, and walk further to reach the railway station. From there, you had to take a train and travel another three and half hours to reach the town. There were separate colleges for women and men. Let Aniyan Namboodiri stay at the lodge near the temple managed by an *embrandiri*. And Thankam in the Women's Hostel. All these arrangements were made by Sahasranamam, the lawyer. The assistant, Sankaran Nair, fetched the bullock cart. Aphan Namboodiri had already left for a distant farmhouse pretending that he did not know anything about these plans. Netyaramma packed Thankam's bedroll and box of clothes. Weighed down by thoughts of separation from her daughter, she alternated between weeping and offering advice by turn. When it was time to set off, Thankam went to the mana. Edathiamma stood beneath the *mandaram* tree, sunk in thought. Dressed in shabby clothes looped about her waist, her hair yanked back and tied into a knot, that slim, pale young woman looked like a mendicant. For a long time, they gazed into each other's eyes silently. They could say nothing. In the end, Edathi said, 'So, Thankam you are leaving. Yes, go. Study well, and come back victorious. How happy I am to see you happy. So, Ettan had the strength to do this. When you return, learned and successful, it will please even Aphan!'

Pausing a bit, she said with a sigh, 'I wonder—will we see each other again! Are we destined to meet at all? I doubt it. However, child, do not forget me. Thankam, I love you more than anyone else in the world. I feel that we are one in body and spirit.'

Thankam could not control her tears. She fell at Edathi's feet, sobbing, 'Forget my sister, my friend, my goddess? Edathi, even if I forget myself, I will not forget you. We will meet in the holidays. I will write to Unni Ettan. Isn't Ettan's deeksha about to end? Edathi … forgive Ettan.'

Tethi Edathi made no reply. She was very calm. Child! May you have a good life. It looked as though she was blessing Thankam with her long, beautiful eyes and regretting that she, Tethi, did not have the self-will that Thankam had shown. As she placed her hands on Thankam's head and blessed her, Tethi's tears fell on Thankam's head, even as Thankam's tears fell on Tethi's feet.

How long did they remain so! She could not remember. To this day, she felt that her head was placed on Edathi's feet. Tethi's hands, cool as lotus stems, calloused from wearing brass bangles, were they still on her head? ...

Mrs Nair patted her own forehead. On that day, for a long time they had stood looking into each other's eyes. Did she think when she said farewell that she would never see her Edathi again? And when they met, even if they did, did she think that they would not recognize each other ...

No one remembers, Edathi ...

Life is like that.

Please forgive me ...

Homecoming

Very slowly, Thankam realized that anything acquired through stubborn insistence might later bring pain. It aroused guilt, which pinched and hurt one's conscience. She had to bear whatever came her way, unable to complain to anyone about it. This became clear to her within a week of joining college. The women's hostel was a small building. Not many students, but most of them, could not adjust to her food or other habits. There were four cots to a room, placed close to each other. No pond to have a bath. No temple to offer worship. Nor even to spend time with one's own thoughts. Still, she managed to dream about her home and relatives. What would Achan and Amma be doing now? She was the only child, after the loss of seven children and after all kinds of penances. Her parents had seen to it that she had known no sorrow. Even if she had asked for the new moon, there were people ready to leap up for it. Perhaps that was why she was so stubborn and self-willed. She recalled how many times Unni Ettan had to persuade her father before he gave his wordless permission for her to study further.

'... I have promised Thankam, Aphan. You must let her go to college. Whatever she studies; be it Sanskrit or English, it would still be learning. It can only bring good. Besides, Aniyan is also there with her. That fellow too insists on studying. Times have changed and we must know it.'

At first, Aphan Namboodiri had exploded. Then he said, 'Unni, if you too are so particular, let it be so. Henceforth, I am not going to bother about her. You take over. Didn't I lose seven children? I shall consider her one last loss. Unni, Manampalli Iraviravi Namboodiri has never yet been defeated. Today, I am defeated. Not by her, but by you.'

'Aphan, this defeat will one day turn into victory,' Ettan insisted. 'She will study and fare well. She will get a better husband than the one you've chosen. On that day, Aphan, you will certainly bless her.'

Even so, when she took leave of her father, the sharp edge of his horrifying and pained gaze pierced Thankam's heart.

'After paying such a price what had she finally gained? Had she gained anything at all?' The question remained in the air. In a way, Thankam's obstinacy turned out to be Aniyan's good fortune and she entered the portals of a college.

From time to time, Aniyettan visited her in the hostel, handing over the money her father sent, and the snacks, pickles, and herbal oils from her mother. He was a man of few words.

'These days Aphan tires easily.'

Or

'Netyaramma was suffering from a cold.'

'Unni Ettan has begun the *Saptaham* reading.'

On one such occasion, amidst such remarks, he said, 'Edathi has gone to her own illam.'

'Why ... when ... when will she return?'

Questions she couldn't ask.

Custom did not permit Aniyan Namboodiri to even meet his Edathiamma. Then how could she expect him to make such enquiries? At first she thought, why not write Unni Ettan a letter? Later, she felt, 'During the Onam break when I return home I shall find out.'

By then Edathi would have returned. She must take a few more books. Vallathol's[22] *Sahityamanjari*,[23] then some books by V.T.,[24] M.R.,[25] and M.P.[26] It was such a pleasure to listen to Edathiamma reciting poetry! Revolutionary songs recited in that soft, melodious voice filled with pathos reduced the listeners to tears. Why was Edathiamma so melancholy? ... She did not know! Even as she, Thankam, did not know how to weep, Edathiamma probably did not know how to laugh.

When she returned with Aniyettan to her village for her first vacation and alighted at the railway station, she saw the bullock cart of the mana waiting for her. On the way, Aniyettan said, 'Thankam, I suggest you first step into the illam and then proceed to your house. Unni Ettan will be waiting for you.'

'Why would he be waiting?' she asked astonished.

Choosing his words carefully, Aniyettan said, 'Haven't you heard that Edathi has run away?'

'*Run away*? Where to? Why?' She was speechless.

'To her own illam—where else, child? It is only to her own illam. Her mother was ill. They sent a messenger. Aphan, Amma, and Muthassi insisted that they would not send the antharjanams of Manampalli illam to the house of outcastes. "In that case, I

[22] Vallathol Narayana Menon, great poet of pre- and post-independent Kerala.

[23] Collection of Vallathol's poems.

[24] V.T. Bhattathirippad was a well-known social reformer of the Namboodiri community who worked for the empowerment of the Namboodiri women.

[25] M.R. Bhattathirippad was a writer associated with the social reform movement of the Namboodiris.

[26] M. Premji was a writer of the social reform movement of the Namboodiris.

too am an outcaste. I *shall* go," said Edathi. Unni Ettan remained silent and glanced at his mother's face and then Edathi's.'

'And then?' she asked breathlessly.

'Then what, Edathi knew her duty. Her mother lay dying. She just wanted to see her once. Her husband and relatives were opposed to that. She stood up, fell at Unni Ettan's feet and then at Mother's and then, paying no attention to anything else, she stepped out and walked away. Aphan and Amma insisted that they would not permit the one who walked out the way Edathi did to return to the illam.'

'So, has Unni Ettan also abandoned her? Is all this going on with Ettan's knowledge also?'

An uncontrollable sob burst from her. Aniyettan remained calm and stroking his head, said, 'Fear not, Thankam. These are not unique events. Very soon, I too will cut this top-knot of mine. Then I will also be declared an outcaste. I am practising patience only because Aphan holds the key to the treasury.'

Glancing at that courageous young man's fearless face she thought, 'Unni Ettan's brother ... How did he turn out like this? Probably a throwback to a previous generation. After all, the formidable Aphan Namboodiri was the brother of the guileless Achan Namboodiri. The same pattern was being repeated. But what of the fate of poor Edathi caught between these two? Would she turn out to be the insane younger aunt, the water-crazy Muthassi, or Kuriyedath Thatri ... Who will my Edathi turn into?'

Choking, she said, 'Aniyettan, I shall go home, have a bath, eat a meal, and then come over. Now, Unni Ettan must be reading the *Bhagavatham*.[27] Let him finish. I have to strengthen my mind before I meet Unni Ettan ...'

---

[27] The sacred book relating the story of Sree Krishna.

When they got down from the bullock cart, Netyaramma was standing guard at the gate itself. At the sound of the bullock's bell, the attendants of the mana and the madhom rushed up.

'Thankam, child, you have lost weight!'

'Oh, child, Thankam, how tall you've grown! ...'

'We've been dying to see you, Thankakutty.'

Amidst all this small talk and welcome, she walked slowly up to Netyaramma where she stood, weeping. The daughter stood before her, as though biting back and swallowing her tears. They had been separated only for four months. But it seemed like four yugas. Thankam, who had not wept even once, fell on her mother's bosom with a sob ...

'Won't father forgive me, Amme? Won't he take pity on me? Won't he bless me?'

Netyaramma stroked her daughter's back and stuttered, 'My beloved daughter! So far I have not seen your dear father forgive anyone. But, now he will be obliged to forgive. He has no other option. But by then will it be too late for forgiveness? ...'

Both of them felt as though a shadow had crossed by the window. Who was it? Who was it that had stood on the other side of the wall listening carefully? Who was it?

'I think His Excellency has arrived after his meals ...' Netyaramma stood up and walked indoors.

That night Thankam had a strange dream. Was it a dream or a visitation? Or a living appearance? Whatever it be, this old woman, Thankam Nair, had never in her life had such an experience. Recalling it, she felt thrilled. On the top storey of the Kacheri Malika, next to the room where her parents slept, there was a small room where she lay. The fatigue of the journey, news of Edathi's flight, Father's protest, her own detachment ... the combined effect of all these emotional turmoils had taken their toll on her mind and body. She did not know right from wrong ...

Her head aching and body perspiring, she lay tired and wilted on the cot next to the small window. In the sky, the cluster of clouds hung heavy. The shooting star shone. An occasional growl of the thunder. Burning oppressive heat. Had she slept or dozed? Or fainted? In any case, her eyes had closed and her body had become still. She thought it was the third quarter of the night. She felt that the door to the room where Father slept was opening slowly. Faint footsteps approached closer and closer. Even though her eyes were closed, she felt someone looking at her fondly. Suppressed breathing. Heavy fingers caressed her forehead lovingly. 'Poor thing, my child, poor thing.' It seemed as though that caress was filled with the rhythm of those words. Slowly, a face lowered itself and lips touched her forehead. She could feel the callus of the forehead marked by prostrations in the temple, and the smoothness of the bald head. Oh! My Achan! She lay there horripilating, having fallen into the waves of an intense, deep bliss. She felt faint with pleasure and barely noticed the sound of those same footsteps receding.

Manampalli Aphan Namboodiri's Nair daughter did not sleep for the rest of that night. As for Father, he would not have slept either. Was Father asking for forgiveness? Or was he forgiving her? Hidden in that dry heart was there such a huge ocean of love? She was very fortunate. She felt fulfilled: Thankam, the lucky woman who got everything.

After her vacation, before she returned to college, she fell at Father's feet and remained there for a long time as though saying, 'Bless me, Father, please forgive me! Your wish is my wish too. I shall never again deny that!'

Oh ... the ways of destiny. How many strange paths does it drive us to take to fulfil our duties. After that occasion, she would never have had this opportunity.

Fate of a Generation

The cool breeze of dawn began to blow. The city slept peacefully. In the street partly illuminated, partly sunk in darkness, shadows moved like the memories of olden days. Mrs Nair wondered whether this was a dream or reality. She rubbed her eyes and looked around. In the lower regions of the northern horizon, the star Dhruva[28] shone unmoving, unblinking. Can it at all move from its fixed point? Or was it this stillness that made people take Dhruva as the path finder?

On the shores of the Ganga, some mendicant was reading and explaining the *Gita* to his disciples:

Dukheshanudwignamana:
Sukheshu Vigataspriha
Veetaragabhayakrodha:
Sthidhadhirmuniruchyate.[29]

The one who is unruffled by pain, who does not seek pleasure, one whose passions have perished, such a yogi can be called a steadfast man of learning ... He will, in future, be freed from the cycle of birth.

[28] Hero of a legendary story, Dhruva gained spiritual stability through penance. The name denotes calm and stability. It is also the name of a star in the sky.

[29] This verse has been taken from the *Bhagavad Gita*, canto 2, verse 56 describing a truly equanimous, spiritual person.

In those days, she did not know whether Unni Ettan was such a steadfast man of learning. But, like the star Dhruva, he was a radiant, unshakeable man. Edathiamma was both lucky and unlucky to get a husband like him. She could not understand him. No one could. Not even Thankam, who had moved very closely with him from early youth. On that day, when she went to the room where books and manuscripts were stored and had stood silently behind him as he sat in a corner in front of the brass lamp reading the Mahabharatam, she could sense this enigmatic aura which enveloped him.

She recalled that Ettan was reading the conversation between Draupadi[30] and Yudhishtira[31] in the *Aranya Kandam*.[32] Having been defeated in the false game of dice and insulted, having given up everything, when they were roaming in the forest, Draupadi asked Dharmajan:[33]

Quoting dharma you gave up the country and the wealth rightfully ours and came here. To practice dharma you suffer and make us all suffer too. In order to uphold the dharma you would even give up your life. This dharma which you practice at great cost, what does it give in return? Please tell me why we should have a dharma which does not protect Dharmaputra himself?

[30] One of the heroines of the Mahabharatam, daughter of King Drupada and wife of the Pandavas.

[31] The eldest Pandava prince.

[32] The chapter from the Mahabharatam describing Pandavas' stay in the forest.

[33] The son of Dharma Raja, the God of Death, the name could also mean the one who observed dharma faithfully. It is another name for Yudhisthira. 'Dharmaputra' means the son of righteousness.

Panchali raised this complaint with the same anger and remon-stration Edathi showed when she talked about Ettan who read Yudhishtira's reply, in a firm voice:

Dharmamacharippen dharmathin
Phalamorthalla Sundari!
Sastram thettichitatheyum
Sadhuvrittangal nokkiyum
Krishne Dharmathil en chittam
Swabhavathal urachatam
Dharmam Kachotamayullon
Dharmishtanmarkku nindyanam.

Oh! Beautiful one! I do not walk the path of Dharma
Dreaming of the results it may bring
Oh, Panchali! Obeying the sastras,
Taking care of the needs of the disadvantaged
Dharma has taken root in my mind
As a part of my behaviour
A person who trades in Dharma
Is hateful to those who follow the path of Dharma.

Had Edathiamma raised such a question Ettan might have given this same kind of reply. When she stood watching that young man immersed in the *dharmic* dilemmas of olden days, she remembered a story Edathi had told her. It was the first Thiruvathira after her wedding. All celebrations had been arranged befitting the status of Manampalli mana. Many guests were expected. Everything, bath, play, and feast, had to be outstanding. Even Muthassi and the mad Cheriyamma were very particular it be so. As the heroine of these festivities held in honour of their wedding ceremony, Edathi was very proud and euphoric! Very early in the morning, before the sun rose, the women made it a point to jump into the pond, leaping, frolicking, and singing.

Dhanumasathil Thiruvathira
Bhagavan thante thirunalane ...
Atenam pol patenam pol
Thutikkenam pol Kukkenam pol.

Thiruvathira of the month of Dhanu
Is the birthday of Bhagavan (the lord) ...
We should dance, sing,
Bathe and splash water.

After the water-play and bath, seeing her Edathi lit by a red-dish glow, dressed in newly washed gold-bordered traditional clothes, her eyes adorned with collyrium, her neck with a garland of *karuka* grass, marking her forehead with sandalwood paste, even Thankam felt like kissing her; she recalled that story with a faint smile. Like Parvathy,[34] who won Shiva,[35] who destroyed the God of Love, Edathi, picking up a hundred-and-one tender betel leaves, went in search of Ettan. On her bare breasts, the thali and other chains glistened. From her hair dropped the ten auspicious leaves.[36]

The main ritual of the the Thiruvathira fast is the preparation of a hundred-and-one betel leaves by women, as an offering for the Goddess. These leaves are prepared personally and shared with

[34] Parvathy, daughter of Himavan (lord of the Himalaya mountain), fell in love with Lord Shiva and did penance to gain him as her husband.

[35] Shiva was in deep meditation, when persuaded by the devas, Kama Deva tried to distract him. Because he was disturbed, an angry Shiva opened his eyes and burnt Kama Deva to ashes.

[36] Considered to be an auspicious gesture to please Bhagavathi (Mother Goddess), women collected these leaves in the month of Karkitakam and wore them in their hair. The juice from these leaves was worn on their foreheads.

their husbands. In the ritual room, where Ettan sat alone, Edathi told Thankam, she had called out to him shyly.

'When you finish, please come over here. I have something to tell you.'

Fanning the smoke over the sacrificial pit with his palm-leaf fan, Ettan said, 'Please wait for a moment. The *Ganapathi homam* is ending. After the *Bhagyasooktham*, I shall come.'

She had mentioned that even though Ettan did not turn to look at her, his sweet voice had thrilled her. As soon as he finished the puja and stood up, she had to hand over the betel leaves. And then she must say, 'Please come to the machu. Together we have to chew these one-hundred-and-one betel leaves today. Not merely these betel leaves, but this whole life has to be enjoyed together.'

Ettan would, at that time, flick her cheeks and laugh. Then ... as she stood sunk in these kinds of soul-stirring thoughts, from the other side boomed his mother's rough voice, 'Unni! *Come here!* If you have finshed the puja, you must eat breakfast and go to the Kacheri Malika. Thankam said that Aphan is calling you ...'

Later, Edathi said that on that day she was angry enough to kill Thankam. Ettan got up and took the betel leaves from her in a routine fashion. And without so much as glancing at her face, he had just walked away. For a long time Edathiamma had stood startled and unmoving. When Edathiamma related this story to her, she could not understand its underlying pathos and disappointment. But, today, when she recalled the clear, sweet tone of the young man reciting from the Puranas, the one who had become a sacrificial goat to dharma, her mind broke with sorrow.

'Unni Etta' ... She had called softly.

He turned and looked at her.

'Oh, Thankam, you're here. When did you come?'

'Just now. I went home, I bathed and came over here. Didn't Aniyettan give you the news?'

Ettan looked slightly sheepish. 'I have not seen Aniyan yet. He might have eaten something as soon as he came in and gone out again. For some days, I have confined myself to this book room, Thankam. I did not even know that you had returned. Actually, I am not aware of any happening.'

She wanted to say, 'Did you ever know what was going on?' But, what she said was:

'The one who always knew when I had arrived, and sent the offerings—she is not here. Perhaps that is why you did not know, Unni Etta.'

Saying nothing, Ettan continued to turn the pages of the book.

Choking up, she asked, 'Etta, where is my Edathi? Have you all forsaken her? The things I hear!'

Once more, Ettan was silent for a while. After that, he rose and turned to face her.

'Thankam, no one can abandon anyone. How can man separate what God has united? I used to say this to your Edathi also, Thankam. For those born into the Brahmin clan, life is a sacrifice. More than one's own pleasure, they will have to accept others' wishes. I was born a Brahmin. And she became my wife. But, we have always differed in our understanding of dharma.'

'*Dharma!* ...' she flared. 'Why are you talking about this dharma at every possible opportunity! The dharma which takes no note of the times, let it go its way. If you were asked to kill your mother, would you, like Parasurama,[37] do that also?'

Unni Ettan remained calm and then shot her a piercing glance. 'Child! I know that the times are changing. But you should not

---

[37] One of the Brahmin sages who is supposed to have retrieved the land of Kerala from the sea. His father Jamadagni suspected his wife of disloyalty and ordered his son to kill her. Parasurama did what he was asked unhesitatingly. Later, when his pleased father told him to ask for a boon, he requested his father to bring his mother back to life.

forget that there are some who do not know that. Have you even once thought about your own father? How sad my Aphan is? How innocent and straightforward. He is stubborn and insists that the views he holds whether right or wrong should win through. If that stubbornness is broken, he will also break. In his whole life, he was defeated but once: by you—no, by me—but since then, his heart has grown feeble. Now, if I defeat Aphan in the matter of Tethikutty also, he won't survive, Thankam. Who will take the responsibility for that sin?'

Thankam stood there, unable to answer. The cruel face of truth had been unveiled. On one side, her father's steely face, strong, stubborn, yet for the time defeated. On the other, a helpless, intelligent, and pure young woman's suffocating face filled with agony. Between the two, the crushed, helpless faces of herself and Ettan ... Whom should she join? Whom could she give up?

Suffering humanity woke in Thankam and she wept, 'Oh Lord! Is this the fate of this generation ... Is this the curse that we received? Is there no way to escape this dharmic dilemma?' She asked, 'We have been told that if Edathi went through the remedial act, father would accept her. Why don't you think about that, Etta? Etta, go to her house just once. Father's obstinacy will slowly melt.'

Unni Ettan said in a very grand voice, 'That would be of no use, Thankam. Even if Aphan agreed, I do not think she will agree. The girl raised by Puthusseri Kuttan cannot live as this illam's daughter-in-law. Besides, we have to think of the succession to the illam also. That is Aphan's argument ... So ...'

'So ...' she asked, 'can a succession to the illam happen without Edathi? Is that something you don't know, Unni Ettan?'

Massaging his hands restlessly, Ettan said, 'I know that. But, Aphan doesn't. That is why I mentioned it. Three or four years have passed since I married Tethikutty. So far, she has not conceived.

Now, she has left the illam and Aphan must be thinking why not arrange a second marriage for me.'

Thankam felt as though she had been slapped.

'And? Etta, did you agree?'

'No, Aniyathi, no. Tethikutty might have a life without me, but I have no life without her. Manampalli Unni Namboodiri might be a traditionalist and a fool. But let her know he is not so cruel as to abandon the wife he wed with fire as witness. Please tell her that ... And, that he knows how to wait for the people he loves.'

Saying this, he walked hastily onto the small path leading to the prayer room.

Thankam did not linger. She had gone to him, her heart full of anger. She returned with her heart full of sorrow. She wished her Ettan had been a crueller person—a selfish man, an impudent man. Then, neither she nor her Edathiamma would have had to suffer such a fate. Filled with a hundred disturbing thoughts, her head bowed, as she was returning through the northern side of the illam, she heard Ettan's mother telling grandmother.

'The one who used to walk around calling herself Netyaramma and preening. Now look at her! The girl who was raised with great care is mixing with those riff-raff Muslim women, dressed in a blouse and sari, not observing either the laws of pollution or untouchablility. Her desire was to convert our own antharjanams to her ways. Because it was Unni, it did not work ... The good fortune of the tharawad ... the good fortune!'

Grandmother said, 'Look here, what we call *Brahmaswam* is fire. Burning fire. If you steal and eat more than your due, it won't work out. Do you know how much has been transferred to Nair veedu, by way of jewellery, money, and property? Everything will catch fire and perish ... burn up ...'

It was her mother that these women were cursing. She pretended she had not heard and walked on. These creatures had never been able to bear Aphan Namboodiri caring for his wife and daughter. And what about their intolerance? They couldn't stand to see their own son looking lovingly at his own wife. She turned and looked at the western storey of Manampalli mana. Had the festering dissatisfactions begun to light the flames there?

At the gate, under the banyan tree, she met Aniyan Namboodiri who asked, 'Thankam, have you met Ettan?'

'Yes.'

'And then, what happened?'

'What can happen? Isn't it all over?'

'No, Thankam, everything is yet to happen. Recently, I met P.K.P., who said, "The volcano is about to burst into lava and flow. Wait and see. You will see what you have not seen till now. And even hear what you have not heard so far."'

Saying this much, Aniyan walked rapidly away. Thankam stood staring. She remembered that it had taken six months for her to understand the meaning of what Aniyettan had said. She had been in the hostel. Very early in the morning when the newspaper arrived, she heard loud laughter and raised voices from the reception room. Some people were saying, 'Is this an antharjanam? I cannot believe it. Would one among them, who usually walks around with head bent, with the umbrella and the shawl, have this much courage?'

Another person said, 'Only they will have this much courage. Because they are the people who have suffered so greatly. Only a volcano can burst like this!'

This comparison to a volcano was P.K.P.'s she thought, startled. That was what Aniyettan had said.

Thankam walked into the reception room.

Holding aloft that day's newspaper, her companion said, 'Thankam, did you see this, an antharjanam has given up the *gho-*

sha and come out. This is the picture of her speaking. Look, Can you believe it?'

Thankam looked. Thankam saw. Under the heading 'From Darkness to Light', a photograph. A woman dressed in a sophisticated manner in a sari and a blouse, head held high, that young woman who stood on the platform, whom did she resemble? Those eyes ... that stance ... Oh, my Edathiamma ... Is that you? Was there a burning volcano inside you? When it burst and scattered, those glowing sparks fell on the surroundings scorching them. As she continued to look at that photograph, Thankam's eyes filled. Tears, of half pride, and half sadness. Like the burning candle, that gaze was filled with heat and glow before the final melting. Devaki Manampalli, who held her head high, and spoke in a firm voice on that day, 'I am not the representative of any one caste, one religion, or one society. I am the representative of the entire clan of women who have, for centuries, endured ill treatment. You can look at this Truth which stands before you, veil cast aside, and bless it or curse it. But, you must remember that this burden of sorrow which is ours is your creation ...'

'This burden of sorrow which is ours,' Thankam said slowly '... hers, Edathiamma's, their mothers, their grandmothers, their combined and accursed burden of sorrow. Will they be able to rid the next generation of it?'

With intense mental turbulence, Mrs Nair sobbed, 'Dear children, please forgive us. The cross, which we bore, may it not fall on your shoulders too. This is the prayer of Devi Bahen, Sumitrananda, and Mrs Nair.'

Last Blessings

Once, many years ago, at midnight, Chengannat temple caught fire—a story Unni Ettan had told her. At the *gopuram* entrance, which was in a disorderly condition after the festival, three of them had been playing: Unni Ettan, Aniyettan, and herself. She was six or seven years old at that time. Aniyettan picked up a firecracker from the premises, covered in withered banyan leaves, elephant dung, and betel-leaf stains and was trying to light it with fire from the temple kitchen.

'No, Aniyan, don't do it. Don't play with fire. If a spark from that falls on this waste heap and ...?'

'Let it all burn. It would be that much cleaner,' insisted Aniyettan.

'What if the sparks falls on the temple and it burns down? The illam too would catch fire. Everything will be destroyed ... It did happen once before.'

Unni Ettan related what had happened during the time of his great-great grandfather. At that time, the roof of the temple had not been copper plated. It was covered only with matted dried coconut leaves. Chengannattappan was the deva who rode on the umbrella of their ancient ancestor grandfather, who had gone on a pilgrimage to Kasi. A god, who answered grandfather's call. Worship at the temple had brought prosperity and fame to Manampalli mana. If, a lamp lit by us at the entrance, went out, the divine beings would light it again. It was at this temple that at midnight people had seen a light above the sanctum sanctorum. At first, the guards thought that it was the glow from lamps lit by the devas. It was later when the flames blazed and they felt its heat that they cried aloud ...

'Chengannat temple is on fire! Come fast! Come running! Run and come!'

Everybody came running. Among them, grandfather too. Around the sanctum sanctorum, the red fire swirled and blazed. Through this red haze shone the idol of Chengannattappan. A granite idol placed in a waist-deep hole and firmly fixed with eight binding materials. How could they save it? Who would be prepared to do that? In the wind that hissed and roared, pieces of wooden rafters burst and scattered. Grandfather stood for a moment, surveying the scene. Then he dashed to the temple pond, immersed himself in it, and rushed back without drying himself. He jumped into the pit of fire, shook the glowing idol loose and carrying it, ran to the prayer room of his illam, placed it there, and fell backward. The source of grandfather's strength? Who but Chengannattappan ...

Later, that temple had been rebuilt. The old rafters were removed and copper slabs hammered in. The deity became more powerful. The illam also prospered.

Aniyettan listened and then asked, 'So, if it burns down again, won't it be rebuilt once more and become more prosperous? So, let it burn ...'

'But, grandfather is not here today,' insisted Unni Ettan. 'Would there ever be another like him? A man who sacrifices himself to protect the gods.'

On that day, she did not remember Aniyettan arguing that God was meant for Man. But, he had burst the firecracker on that very spot. At that startling sound, she remembered how the bats that hung from the banyan tree and the crows had flown away in confusion.

Today, where and on which sanctum sanctorum, had this fire-cracker fallen, thrown by Devaki Manampalli? Will they be able to save the God? Were there people who were strong enough? ... She knew that only if some of the outdated customs and beliefs were destroyed, could something new be built in their place? And when those new customs become outdated, they too may have to be changed. The revolutionaries of the previous generation equated God with certain ideals. Freedom of the country, freedom of the individual, freedom of the society ... sacrificing oneself for these ideals was their life. She was happy that Tethi Edathi had used her own life as a firecracker and burnt the debris surrounding her. But what of Unni Ettan? The god installed in that sanctum sanctorum! Like the ancestor of old, would he be able to carry the chosen deity to a safe place? The revolution of Nair Veettil Thankam attending college was forgotten. Also forgotten was that Aniyan Namboodiri had sheared off his top-knot. The act of a Namboodiri woman dis-carding her veil and emerging into the open, overshadowed every previous shocking act that broke social codes. Mrs Nair remem-bered how soon fame rose or declined. Those were the days when not a single newspaper failed to carry a photograph of Devaki Manampalli. No meetings without her speeches. People travelled long distances just to see her, greet her, and to praise her.

'In the town hall today, Mrs Manampalli is speaking. Aren't you going, Thankam?' Her companions in the hostel would ask.

'No. I have a headache,' she would excuse herself. In her pres-ent condition, how could she face Edathiamma? Those weeping eyes would be glowing. Those pale cheeks quivering. This Devaki Manampalli, who moved like a tempest, shattering every obstacle in the path of 'progress,' who was she to her? ... The weak, tortured Tethi Edathi, whom her dear Unni Ettan had wedded and brought home? ... No, no, no. Her mind repeated in pain. She was not Unni Ettan's; she belonged to the society. To the country, Tethi Edathi had been elevated from an individual to a movement.

For some reason, Thankam felt uneasy. She did not go to her village during that vacation. When Aniyettan came to escort her, she said, 'Ettan, I have a great deal to study. I won't be able to do anything at home. Things there would be turbulent. Tell father that I shall come after my examinations.'

Aniyettan also agreed, 'You are right, Thankam! Everything is in a mess at the illam. Aphan spends his time scolding and fighting with whomever he meets, and is preparing for a ritual outcasting of Edathiamma. All the old women are cursing and scolding Edathiamma. Ettan alone does not step out of the library. Only when they made preparations for a second marriage, he said, "No, I will not marry again. Aphan! After all, there is Aniyan. He will take care of the succession plans of the illam."'

Mrs Nair remembered how quickly human desires broke and crumbled. The young girl, Thankam, had decided that she would study, become independent, pass MA or MSc, and become a high-ranking career woman. Devaki Manampalli had dreamt that she would uplift society and make it free. The revolutionary, P.K.P. Namboodiri, had decided that he would become a martyr, building a beautiful and equal world. Out of these, some, or maybe quite a few, had been achieved. But what happens when the fruit bursts and scatters, leaving only the skin behind, when dreams are partially achieved? What happens to the people? In those days, ideals were life itself. They were euphoric. They had obstinately felt that they would certainly win whatever they struggled for. That was what powered life. She was convinced that this soft-hearted antharjanam, Tethikutty, with moist eyes and hushed voice, could not remain Devaki Manampalli for long. She would return. To her own house, to her husband's heart. Once more, there would be an installation of a bride in the inner courtyard of Manampalli illam. Time reconciles everything. This wedded pair should be reunited. Make them agree. She would tell Unni Ettan, 'Ettan, when I return from college, I will visit a particular place on my way home. I will bring someone else when I return. Be prepared to wear the thattu and the shoulder cloth, and be ready once more.'

She would write to Edathi:

For the information of the social worker, Devaki Manampalli. I know that you have seized and are holding my Edathi, the young antharjanam, Tethikutty. I want her back. I, Thankam, am coming over. You have to once again wear the mantrakodi and the veil, and step down with me ...

Imagining Ettan and Edathi living together happily, she rejoiced.

But everything ended as wishful thinking, disappearing into thin air like daydreams. Two days before the examination, Aniyettan arrived in great haste. Calling out to her, who was studying hard, he said, 'Thankam, er ... there is nothing to worry ... but, er ... We have to go back soon to our village. A telegram came saying that Aphan is not doing too well. There is a car waiting. Let us go soon.'

Aniyettan's tone held a frightening, stuttering quality. For a moment, she stood immobile, and then ran forward with a long wail. Without washing her face, combing her hair, nor even changing her sari, she climbed into the car. The car ran on. Where was it going? To the other end of the world? ... To the netherworld ... or to the edge of the horizon? Running, running, wearily, she should in the end fall into her father's lap. She wanted to lean on that loving bosom. Ask for his forgiveness. No, her father would not brush her aside. She was not a Sudra girl. Her father was not a Brahmin. No caste system could separate them. They were connected by the divine father and daughter bond, which guides the great creator Brahma[38] or even the smallest atom.

She could cobble together what happened during that journey or when she arrived, only from what others told her later.

Aphan Namboodiri's ailment came on quite suddenly. He had fallen unconscious in the bathing ghat. Someone had picked him up and brought him to the mana. Both the doctor and the apothecary reached him immediately. They instantly commenced the religious offerings and special healing mantras. People from surrounding regions heard the news and assembled at the mana. But Aphan had lost his speech. Once in a while, as he regained consciousness, he looked about him, at people who stood around him; his lips moved and he tried to speak. But, he never spoke again.

Weeping, Netyaramma explained the details of the illness to the doctor.

Thankam was told that in the days before his illness, father had been very uneasy. His habitual bursts of temper in any exchange had diminished. He was not even interested in the affairs of the mana. When the assistants pressed him for answers, he would say, 'Ask Unni. Henceforth, he is in charge.'

If Unni Namboodiri asked him something, he would say, 'I think my time is over, Unni. From now on, you do whatever you want.'

He never said much even to Netyaramma. Once when she questioned him, he said, 'Ammalu, take Thankam and go home. I have saved enough for you to manage on. Also, Thankam is studying. Please tell her that this father of hers is a worthless fellow.

---

[38] One of the gods in the Hindu trinity—Brahma, Vishnu, and Shiva—who are entrusted with the functions of creation, preservation, and destruction (coinciding with birth, life, and death in human life).

He never once petted his own daughter. All his attention was on managing household affairs. Even so, Ammalu, Thankam meant everything to me. Ammalu, everything. Her future can only be good.'

Netyaramma wept. Never had she heard such words from Aphan Namboodiri. He was strong-minded and powerful, mentally and physically. At his resounding voice, the surroundings used to tremble. But, when he felt that he was overpowered by the younger generation, his spirit broke. He had heard the news of Tethikutty from various people. His efforts to outcast her did not succeed. Nor could he persuade Unni to remarry. During that time, he was defeated in some court cases concerning tenancy rights. On top of everything else, and worst of all, some people led by Aniyan attempted to arrange for lower castes to enter the Chengannat temple.

Of late, he had had bouts of giddiness and fainting spells. Netyaramma begged him, 'Please consult the apothecary. Or let's go to the well-known doctor in town.'

But Aphan would not agree to anything. In the end, people carried him in from the steps of the temple tank.

Thankam arrived to see Aphan Namboodiri lying on the wooden cot placed in the outer verandah of the illam. Seated at his head, Unni Ettan was taking care of him. In the outer verandah, the inner verandah, and courtyard, relatives, tenants, and assistants thronged. When Thankam saw Netyaramma sitting quietly in a corner of the verandah wiping her nose, she understood for the first time how insignificant they were in this house. Her beloved father was on his deathbed. They could neither touch him, nor take care of him, nor even approach him. This man was no one to them, nor they to him. Netyaramma hugged her daughter and wept, 'My beloved daughter, it's all over for us ... everything ... every single thing ... '

When Aphan Namboodiri regained consciousness, Thankam approached him and bending low, she addressed him, 'Father! My father! ...'

He looked at her carefully. Did he recognize her? His lips moved. Was he calling her ' 'My beloved daughter?' Or just saying 'Thankam?' There was no sign of a curse in those eyes. Instead, there sparkled the glow of blessings. In all their lives, they had never once spoken so eloquently. Aphan caught hold of Unni Ettan's hand and placed it on his lap. Thankam stood reaching out to him. Did he imagine that he had carried her hand and linked it with Unni Ettan's? A whistling sound pierced Thankam's ears. Shadows swung. The light faded. That she had fainted and fallen onto Aphan Namboodiri's chest, that he had held her shoulders with his left hand—it was reported to her because an important purification ritual had to be held.

She did not remember when she regained consciousness—was it night or day, was it several days later? Inside, she could hear chanting. Outside, the sound of wood being cut for the pyre.

Netyaramma hugged her daughter and said, 'Get up, Thankam. Our relationship with Manampalli mana is over. Come, let us go.'

She had wept, 'Amme, where is Achan? Show me my Achan ...'

'Now, we cannot step in, my child. We would pollute the house. Even otherwise, polluted or not, he left with your touch on him. What a disaster ...'

When she knew that she could not even see her father's body, she slapped her head and wept profusely.

The rituals were being delayed because custom demanded that before the last rites began, the Nair wife and children had to leave. But Thankam paid no attention to it. Finally, Unni Ettan had said in an imposing voice, 'Thankam, do you know something? The one who left us was your father. To me, he was everything. Our grief is the same. But, child, shouldn't we respect the customs of the village? Do go now. Aphan is dead. But I am here for you. Your Unni Ettan. Please remember that.'

In the most important moment of her life, she realized something significant. The house in which she had been born and raised was not hers. She could not claim her father as her own. Nothing was hers. They had no rights in this house. When she straightened her clothes and got into the car, a single question remained foremost in her mind. Where to? ... Where to ... Where to ...?

The boat of life had finally landed in this ghat, thought Mrs Nair. Turning Devaki Manampalli into a yogini and Mrs Nair into a pilgrim, why had fate brought them together?

For several days after her father's death, she had been like a mad woman. No bathing, no eating, no sleeping. Her mind was caught in a frozen nothingness. A moment of heightened emotion can also contain the quality of no emotion.

Netyaramma was a pragmatic woman. This was nothing new for a woman of the Nair veedu. They had always been the mistresses of a Namboodiri or a thampuran. Bear children. In the end, give up everything and return to their own houses. Large tharawad with many members. Old traditions and disciplines. The wife of the head of the household ruled, her flag flying. So, Netyaramma would have to leave Nair veedu one day, just as she had left Manampalli mana. Such was the fate of *marumakkathayam* families everywhere. She had consciously amassed sizeable wealth. Thankam should never be in need, alone, abandoned, or orphaned.

However hard her mother persuaded her, Thankam never returned to college. Nor did she write the examination. Her obstinacy and selfish longing vanished. Her mind retained only Father's withered face and the eyes that had blessed her. She, who had collapsed, unable to touch his extended hand. Father! Please bless me that I may be born as your daughter in my next birth too. At that time, there will be only one caste in the world. Father and daughter should be able to touch one another. Quoting decadent customs, people will not be allowed to inflict pain on others.

When her thoughts reached this stage, she shivered. Memories shattered; when had she become Mrs Nair? Oh! ... yes—a few days after father's death, a young man working somewhere in north India had come home. He came searching for a beautiful and educated woman from a wealthy and famous house. Thankam qualified. They suited each other. Everything was decided very quickly ... No one came from father's illam to attend the wedding. Unni Ettan was performing a year-long deeksha for Aphan. Aniyettan had gone somewhere after his examinations.

Thankam wrote to Edathiamma, 'Your younger sister named Lakshmi and called Thankam is about to become Mrs Nair. On that very day, we leave for his place of work. When I come back next, I hope to see you and Ettan together at father's illam. Please give me your blessing.'

Even today, she was begging for that blessing. Edathi, you denied me your blessings all these years. As though pleading, she fell on the ground, shivering.

Devaki Bahen

Dum, dumdir... tthim ... Dum dir ... Tthim ... Tthim ...

From the distance, a thunderous sound reverberated like war drums. Following that, a gunshot. Tumultuous cheers from slogans raised. The sound of people marching like soldiers. *Tup ... tup ... tup ...* In the end, the sweet melody of bells, and the chanting of Veda mantras. The world was twirling and spinning. Was she fainting? Or had she drifted into a final sleep or death? Her inner consciousness had entered a sphere where there was no difference between pleasure and pain. How long had she been like this? She did not know. She woke to the caress of a very soft hand.

'Ammumma, grandmother! What happened to grandmother? Father! She isn't responding to me!'

'It is nothing, dear child. The long journey has made Ammumma very tired. No sleep at night. And, isn't she old? Tired ... very tired. Let her sleep.'

'Ever since she saw that sannyasini yesterday, Ammumma has not said a word. Father, was she some sort of sorceress? Did you see the look she gave us? Piercing. Who is she, Father?'

'Who knows who she is, child? There are so many sannyasis and sannyasinis in the Himalaya. They have no names, houses, or relatives. She probably looked like someone dear to Ammumma.'

Mrs Nair gradually became aware of her surroundings. She who had last stood on the terrace; how had she come to be on this cot, under this covering? Her head was spinning. She had tried to sit down and gripped a chair. She might have even fallen, or, on hearing the noise, Appu must have rushed in, lifted her up and placed her on the cot, and covered her with a woollen shawl. The pungent odour of some medicine lingered in the room. It was a good thing that her son was a doctor. When he packed a box of medicines she had said, 'Appu, we don't need this when we go on a pilgrimage. Bhagavan will take care of us. He will suffice.'

'Then I too am a Bhagavan,' he said with a smile.

She wanted to say, 'Yes, Appu, you are my Bhagavan. I continue to live through you and in you.' But, much as he loved her, no son could ever understand his mother completely. To him, she was only a mother. A woman is not just a mother. She has many other aspects besides. The tastes and preferences of different generations may not coincide.'

'Ammumma!' Devu used to ask, 'Why did you give me this old-fashioned name? Devu, Devaki. I feel ashamed to even say it to outsiders. I am going to change it to Devika.'

'Child, there is only a difference of two vowels between the names Devaki and Devika. But that is a big difference. Do you know in whose memory I clung stubbornly to this name? I had given my word to someone that I'd name the first child of my first born "Devaki", if it was a girl. Beloved daughter! She had craved greatly for a child and used to say, "Thankam, I do not think I will ever have a child. But your child will be mine too. If it is a girl, give her my name. Or to your child's child."'

It was a time when Thankam was averse to the very idea of marriage itself. But she had pressed Edathi's palms with hers and promised her. 'If one of us has a child, it will belong to both of us.'

In the years of carefree youth, how many such promises are exchanged before people part. Could they all be fulfilled? She had become pregnant four or five years after her marriage. She remembered that for the first delivery, she had not gone home at all.

Saying that there was no hospital there and no one to take care of her, she had brought her mother to her city-home. She had learnt a great deal of what had happened in her village through her mother.

Manampalli mana had been partitioned. The illam was Aniyan's. Unni Ettan had shifted to the bathing house. He had not remarried despite great pressure. Instead, it was Aniyan who married. Aniyettan's wife wore a sari and blouse. She went for public meetings and cinemas and never observed the principles of pollution. Untouchables were allowed into the inner verandah of the mana. Even so, Aniyan's mother and younger aunt had not uttered a word of protest because Aniyan Namboodiri knew how to keep people in their places.

In a voice filled with disappointment, Netyaramma had said, 'Thankam, the mana's generosity and dharma have perished. Aniyan is a very powerful person. He has a car, a factory, and an elephant. I hear that he is going to stand for the next election. But he has stopped the rituals such as the giving of gruel to the poor people, feasts at the temple, and offerings of buttermilk in summer. He thinks that alms-giving is a sin. Poor Unni does not know how to react to what he sees. It seems he went to the gateway of Chengannattappan, prostrated and prayed, "My Viswambharan! Give me the courage! The courage to bear any suffering." After that, he gave everything that belonged to him to Chengannattappan's sanctum sanctorum. In return, all that he gets every day is a single measure of rice. That's what he lives on.'

At this Thankam's eyes filled. 'Mother! Let's ask Edathi to return? Wouldn't she, when she hears of Ettan's condition? Is she that hardhearted?'

'Where is your Edathiamma? She has gone missing for so many days. Didn't you know?' Continuing, she described that story.

After Aphan Namboodiri's deeksha was over, Aniyan went to Puthusseri Illam and requested Edathi, 'Honourable sister-in-law!

Please come back. After you left, Ettan has been behaving like a mad man. Besides bathing, chanting, religious rituals, and worshipping at Chengannat temple, he does nothing. He's not interested in managing the affairs of the family, so I am going to stop studying and take over the affairs of the tharawad. There is no one to take care of household affairs and Amma is very old. Forget whatever has happened. Let us start anew.'

'I shall come, Aniya. For Ettan's sake, I shall walk a great distance backwards. But, for my sake, Ettan too simply has to come forward a great deal. At this stage, it is impossible for me to be the old Tethikutty Antharjanam, carry an umbrella, and walk with my head bowed. I will attend meetings. I will deliver speeches. I will not observe pollution. Would Ettan and Amma approve? Will your own people agree to all this? We should not become the topic of gossip and idle talk within the illam itself. If Ettan himself requests me, I shall return. But I will not do any acts of atonement. Tell him I said this. If he agrees, I shall return.'

Aniyan remarked that as she said these words, the thali tied firmly around Devaki Manampalli's neck had shivered and glistened. In those days, the term 'yes' had a great deal of power. But Unni Ettan did not say the word. If he did, how different destiny would have been! He must have been conscious of his wife's pride and her unwillingness to compromise. Or, it could be because he knew only too well his own weak and submissive nature. He did not have the capacity to break away from the circle of his mother and traditions. So, the eldest scion of Manampalli mana did not attempt to bring his antharjanam back.

'This can be said in a reverse manner too. I am willing to descend. Ask Edathi to ascend a great deal. She left on her own, all by herself. She can also come back unaccompanied. Can't she?'

Aniyan Namboodiri laughed scornfully, 'Ettan, your *Karkitaka-vyazham* has probably not peaked. But Manampalli illam must have children. I am going to marry.'

He married a sophisticated girl with a huge dowry.

Afterwards, all that her mother had said on several occasions, rose one by one to the top of her mind. A tempest that arose from the passion for social welfare, swirled, and struck the land. Many trees, which had stood in the path of progress, fell. Many houses perished. The path was ready. Revolution bore several lives on its wings and took them forward, but it soon became sadly and clearly evident that no tempest could last for ever. With the same speed that it had arrived, the huge wave began to recede. When the euphoria of the early days died down, many people rushed to play their own survival games. People murmured among themselves. Meetings and newspapers ceased to function. Those who were inclined to join political parties began to move in that direction. Others became even more conservative than they had been before. Many antharjanams who had given up their seclusion, retrieved their traditional umbrellas, covered themselves with shawls, and roamed the temples and pilgrimage spots. The situation of some young men who had been ready to die for the society, was pathetic.

P.K.P. Namboodiri's situation was really tragic. Having got involved in social service and public good, his wealth had dwindled. In order to escape multiple wives and their dowries, he married a poor girl and had four or five children. All his special friends from his earlier days abandoned him. The poor man suffered intensely!

Devaki Manampalli did not have a nest to return to. She had also grown larger than any nest. Edathi was the kind who loved freedom more than her own life. She understood that if society wanted freedom, the country had to be free. Edathi was living in some distant ashram as the disciple of Mahatma Gandhi.

Netyaramma continued, 'It would now be futile for her to return. She is a changed person. She does not observe pollution and non-pollution. She cannot cover herself up again because she has been too open. Nor has she any concern about caste. Will it be possible for her to submit to young master Unni's desires? Tethikutty is now an important person. I heard the other day, from those who went to Sevashram, that the name of Devi Bahen was regarded with great respect by even Gandhi and Nehru.'

She sighed, 'So, Tethi Edathi, who turned into Devaki Manampalli, has now become Devi Bahen. She has grown from the social to the national level. Now it is impossible for her to return.'

Thankam had, at that time, thought that everything with regard to Tethi Edathi had come to an end and that she had started a new life. The birth of her son. A promotion for her husband. The responsibilities of a new life. Involving herself in all that, she was not aware of the passage of time. She was happy. Contented. There was no time to think about relationships from a past era.

At times, when she looked through the newspapers, she would read that a satyagraha movement was about to commence in some place. Somewhere else, peace talks were being negotiated. Leaders were arrested. Several people were killed by gunfire. And so on. Mrs Nair thought shamefully that as far as she was concerned, all this news was no different from reading a detective novel. After Amma's death, even the fragile relationship with her village came to an end. Nothing was done consciously, Edathiamma. Nor did they happen on account of our mistakes. Life is like that. Wherever the waves take us, we journey to those different shores, shifting from one place to another. We build a nest and then part. Otherwise, throughout the many journeys you undertook, why didn't you even once think about this young sister 'Thankam'? How many occasions had there been when we reached so close to touching each other and were then parted? During all those occasions, neither Edathi nor I ever raised a little finger to touch each other. Finally, at the last stages of the journey in this tirthaghat, we sit and count memories ... O!

Mrs Nair opened her eyes and looked up. Above her, the ceiling fan rotated at top speed.

Protests and Reprisals

Our epics speak about a bird, a special kind of eagle, named Garudan. That bird, the vehicle of the Lord, flies, circling the heavens. The higher he flies, the better his view of the sights below. So too are memories. As time passes, they become clearer.

She recalled an incident in the year 1942. The flames of the fires of war had towered within and outside the country. The time when the Quit India Struggle[39] was declared, most of the leaders were in jail. Curfew laws were broken. With gunshots, lathi charges, and incendiary actions, the entire country had transformed itself into a battlefront. On the one side, the police with their guns, lathis, and tear gas, in pursuit of a callous manhunt. On the other, helpless people, their only weapons, their will power and burning desire for freedom. For the viewers, the confrontation between the two, a horripilating sight.

In those days, she watched many sights, seated in one of the upper-storey flats of the great city they lived in.

It was the time when martial law had been declared in the city. Not more than four people could gather anywhere. Slogans were not to be raised. Processions were prohibited. The police and the

[39] In 1942, Gandhiji launched a satyagraha movement called Quit India Struggle wherein he demanded that the British should leave India. This was his ultimate demand to the imperial powers to obtain freedom for India. He inspired his followers with the principle of 'Do or Die' while fighting for India's total independence.

army kept constant vigil in the streets. No sound other than the roar of the police vans could be heard. Dawn was just breaking, and above the apartment building in front, a veil of mist had fallen. She had just woken up. Through the window curtain, she looked out idly. The uninteresting road lay stretched like a python with its mouth and nose secured. There were no horse carts, cars, or pedestrians. Not even the loud call of milk vendors. Like the stillness before an earthquake, everything stood startled, immobile.

Suddenly, from the road which led from the main street to the clock tower, came resounding calls. From hundreds of soft throats, the sound of cheers in unison—

Bharat Mata ki Jai! ... Mahatma Gandhi ki Jai! ... Quit India! ... Quit ... Quit ... Quit India!

Dressed in red shirts, red shorts, and red hats, waving the tri-coloured flag came a group of young children who looked like small birds. She had heard that the children below sixteen of the city had united to form a revolutionary organization called 'Valorous Vanara Platoon'. There were reports that the children of the poor and the rich, of kings and common people, and the sons of high-ranking officers had all joined this group. People said that the innumerable rebel organizations in all parts of the country were united by these enthralling youngsters of the new generation. She remembered the great difficulty with which she had sent her children, Appu and Madhu, to the village to prevent them from joining this organization. Mrs Nair had, at times, wondered anxiously whether they too would be organizing these secret societies in the village.

Following the Vanara Platoon came the women from the Narisevasamithi[40] in white khaddar homespun saris and white blouses, singing freedom songs.

[40] A regional women's organization for service to humanity.

Behind them, reciting the slogan 'Freedom or Death', came the courageous young men who had surrendered themselves to the service of the country, those brave youngsters of the Martyr's Group.[41]

The atmosphere reverberated with the sound of slogans, the hissing of police vans, and the rhythm of freedom songs.

'Let me go.'

'Leave me alone!'

'No, we can't let you ...'

'You cannot enter ...'

In this manner, confronting each other, the police and the volunteers were playing a tiger-and-leopard game. In between, someone pointed to the top of the clock tower and screamed, *'Ayyo!* Look there! He ... he ... that child! ...'

A charming, twelve-year-old boy, clutching the freedom flag to his chest, was scaling that towering building. In a voice that could startle the skies, he was crying aloud, *'Bharat Mata ki Jai!'*

The policemen pointed their guns and ordered, 'You fool! Get down, or we will bring you down!'

He looked down and smiled scornfully. His eyes blessed the soldiers as well as the crowds thronging below. Then, hugging the wall, he began the difficult climb along that tricky slope. The red rays of the early morning sun touched the upper parts of the clock tower, smearing them with the colour of blood. Red khaddar shirt, red khaddar shots, ruddy cheeks. He looked like the child of the Sun God, who had snapped off and fallen from the lap of the sky. As he climbed along the smooth roof, if he missed a single step or was distracted, he would fall to his death.

'No, son, no! Get down!' She wanted to call out and warn him.

---

[41] A group of young men who had dedicated their lives to the freedom of their country and were willing to die for their beliefs.

People waited with bated breath. The mother who gave birth to this child was indeed a very lucky woman. And the country which bore her, a proud one.

Carrying the blessings of thousands of people, the boy climbed higher and higher. He reached the top of the building and looked at the crowds of people below, waved his arms, and laughed. He unfurled the national freedom flag and fixed it high up. Slogans that reached the ends of earth continued:

Bharat Mata ki Jai! ...
Veerakumar ki Jai! ...

Next to that tricoloured flag, its wings outspread and moving like the pride of India, stood the boy like a victorious Abhimanyu.[42] Suddenly, police guns roared. Cartridges flew, hissing like a thousand bolts of lightning rising together to the sky ... The angel who stood on the clock tower laughing, trailed blood and twirling, fell on the ground like a small bird.

Tumultous roars. Following that, a confrontation between the people and the police. Lathi charges! Gunshots! People shouting, 'He is ours! We want him! He ... India's Veerakumaran!'

The perimeter surrounding the clock tower was under heavy police security. But pushing aside the throngs of people, a young woman from the Narisevasamithi crept forward. Thrusting aside the policemen, she gathered the boy in her arms. Life had not completely drained from that body, which looked like a tired lotus stem. She held him to her chest and kissed him. The blood flowing

---

[42] A character from the Mahabharatam. Son of Arjuna, one of the Pandava princes. He led the Pandava army single-handed when his elders were not present and was able to break through the Chakravyuha formation devised by Drona, the guru of the Kauravas and Pandavas. Abhimanyu was killed because he did not know how to break out of the Chakravyuha.

from his heart turned her white sari red. Like Bharat Mata, who both smiles and weeps, that young woman's face, seemed to glow with grandeur. The police tried to take the child from her. From her head, wounded by the blows of lathis, blood streamed. The sky itself reddened; it was pierced and fragmented. Even after the policemen had dragged her along the ground, she held the child's body close to her heart. That young woman whose thick eyelashes showed not a single tear drop, from whose forehead blood streamed, from whose eyes fire blazed, and lips quivered, held her head high. That likeness, that glance, whose was it ... whose was it?

Even today, when Mrs Nair thought about this scene, she felt faint again. How weak and petty was she? On that day, why hadn't she run down and entered the throngs of people and said, 'I too am an Indian. I too am with you. That child belongs to me too. Include me also, sister.'

Pleasure is a mesmeric state of euphoria, Mrs Nair thought. There is no quick relief from it. Even so, that evening when her husband returned home, she had asked, 'Did that woman die?'

'Which woman?'

'That woman who fell down under the lathi blows this morning. That woman, who rushed into the midst of the crowds carrying the boy's body—that woman?'

He laughed loudly, 'Oh ... that ... How many women fall beneath the lathi and die. They are even raped. Will we ever know what happened to them? There is no need to know either.'

Later, she heard the news from a police official, her husband's friend. 'Oh! Devi Bahen, she did not die. But four or five women who were her friends were crushed by police brutality. Devi Bahen lay unconscious in the jail hospital for several days. After that, she must have returned to the Sevashram itself. Or, did she get involved in some other lathi charge and die! I do not know anything.' Later, she managed to get more news from him. Devi

Bahen was an inmate of Gandhiji's ashram. She was a woman from Kerala who had achieved a great name in social service activities. Gandhiji's beloved follower.

She trembled. Devi Bahen meant Devaki Manampalli, Tethi Edathi. Was she this woman? She had longed to go and visit Edathi at the ashram. But her husband would not let her. He believed that it would adversely affect his official position. Besides, no one here knew exactly where she was.

After freedom was won, she had not seen Devi Bahen among the people who had come forward quoting the price for their suffering during the struggle. She did not become a minister. Nor even a leader. Nor, on a smaller scale, a committee member. But that unselfish courageous heroine bathed in blood, who had stood holding the symbol of future India close to her chest, she came to Mrs Nair's attention once or twice more.

The woman who travelled with the apostle of non-violence in eastern Bengal during the time of communal riots had a strange resemblance to Devaki Manampalli.

The description of the mother who worked in an ashram in Madhya Pradesh for the upliftment of village women also bore this resemblance. Thankam's husband, on watching her, seeking this resemblance in many women all over India, would say, 'This is an illusion, Thankam. A strange mental disorientation. Your mind is so focused on her that anyone whom you see becomes her.'

Today, in the case of Sumitranandasaraswathi, did that same disorientation sieze her? No, Tethi Edathi, this time I will not let you go. Devaki Manampalli has no liberation from Thankam Nair. We are two faces of this era. The younger generation has two mothers. Won't you accept our children?

Renunciation

Kalyani Devi, an elderly Malayali, used to visit Mrs Nair's house to teach her children Hindi. Inspired by Gandhiji's call to join the National Freedom Struggle movement, she had left her village. She had lived in Wardha for many years. She used to wear only self-woven clothes, using the yarn she had herself spun. Once a day, she ate unsalted, half-cooked rice. In her rare hours of leisure, she chanted the name of Rama. Thankam's children had looked down on this eccentric woman, the way she sat, walked, and chanted, and had laughed at her. 'Mad woman', was their title for her. Kalyani Devi was the kind of woman who was unaffected by any kind of sarcastic or insulting remarks. She lived in some small hut in the Bhangi colony.

'Kalyani Devi, don't you have any relatives in your village? Why stay alone by yourself in your old age?'

'The whole of India is my village. All of you are my relatives. Then why should I be scared?' she had laughed.

'That is not what I asked. Don't you have your own house, relatives, or siblings?' Thankam explained.

For a long time, Kalyani Devi sat silently, meditating before she spoke, 'Mrs Nair, this feeling of "ownership" is just one's imagination. No one is owned by anyone. Even we don't belong to ourselves. Do you know how sannyasis offer their souls? With their own hands they place the pindam at their feet. Thereafter they consider themselves dead. They begin to live for others. I had a friend like that, a woman who took up sannyasam. But I have not placed my own pindam at my feet. The whole of this great country India is my own. All the people in India are my own. You give me a meal a day. I am content with that. But I am tired, Mrs Nair. Seeing and hearing what is happening around us now, I am tired of life.'

As if speaking to herself and with deep sorrow, she said, 'My India, my own country, the *Ramarajyam* which I earned by giving up my life, when I think of its present fate, I feel sad. Today's India is the symbol of all that we had opposed. Theft, black marketeering, internal conflicts, power games—these occupy the centre stage. Mrs Nair, do you know what I saw on the way here? The daughter of a famous freedom fighter who gave up his life for the country's freedom, emerging from a five-star hotel completely drunk, clinging to the shoulders of a foreigner. She was almost naked. As soon as she saw me, she laughed, "Hello, Kalyani Devi ... Come on! Come with me. My father died of hunger. They hanged him. I will enjoy life to the fullest and then die. A death in free India. Come. Come with me."'

As she staggered away, hanging on to that foreigner, I wept. Why wonder at people like Devi Bahen taking to sannyasam?'

'Devi Bahen?' ... After so many days, once again, the name of Devi Bahen. Controlling her turbulence and inner agony, she asked, 'Who is Devi Bahen, Kalyani Devi? Do you know her? Where is she?'

The elderly woman shook her head, 'It is like asking me whether I know myself. Is there anyone who does not know that Amma from the Sevashram? After Gandhiji, there was only her to take on others' sins and atone for them. Her story is very unusual. Someday, someone will write about it. It has to be written. It is that unique.'

Listening to our conversation, all the children of the house came and sat around us. They said that they would like to hear that story which should be written. It looked as though Kalyani Devi also wanted to share her thoughts with someone. 'You know, Mrs Nair, the state of affairs in our native place when we were growing up. If we talk about it, these children will not believe us. They'll make fun of us. For them, it would seem like stories of *yakshi*s. Were women allowed, in those days, to step out of their houses, talk to strangers, or go to school? Could Nair, Ezhavan, Namboodiri, and Christian touch without polluting each other? The bonded labourers had to remain subjugated to the orders of the landowners. The common people had to obey what the king ordered. And the king, in turn, had to obey the sovereign ruler. Men ill-treated women; the young men were assaulted by the heads of their households. Society was oppressed by traditional customs. A country which was the sum total of all these was subjugated by powerful white rulers. Everyone suffered all kinds of oppressions.

'It was at such a time that Gandhiji appeared on the scene. He revealed to us the true picture of the country and said, "Come, if you listen to what I say, I shall give you Swaraj. We can put an end to the injustices. We can gain freedom." He had three conditions—Truth, Equality, and Self-sufficiency. We were people who had promised to preserve these. For that, we destroyed foreign goods. We popularized Swadeshi. We gave up selfishness. But, Mrs Nair, look what has happened after we gained freedom. Even your Devu is wearing a skirt made of foreign cloth, which would have been bought in the black market. How could people like Devi Bahen tolerate seeing such things? She was unable to pardon even a small mistake committed by a young woman at Mahilashram. Not surprising to those who know her.'

Devu said, 'Anything that the teacher says, contains an old-fashioned preachy speech. To her, everything was good and truthful in the olden days, and bad and untruthful in the present day.

All right. Tell us the story of Devi Bahen. We are seated here to listen to that.'

Kalyani Devi moved her head slowly. Then, tapping her lips with her finger, she said slowly, 'It is very difficult to relate everything in an orderly compiled manner. After all, it is not a novel or an epic. It is a story of a real event. A story which happened many times in many places. Much of it has been collected from guesses and the information given by third persons. When we talk of a goddess-like woman, there should be no exaggeration at all. That is what I think. Most probably, you would say that even this is a cooked-up story. Still, it does not matter. Listen. There are certain real events which are stranger than cooked-up stories. This is also one among them.'

Then, Kalyani Devi related the story, which can be summarized thus. 'Devi Bahen was a woman who came from a very good family of Kerala. She had money, honour, and a husband. She gave it all up, intoxicated by the idea of serving the country. Bappuji had put her under severe tests. He sent her to repair small huts, for taking care of Harijans.[43] Kept her in the ashram, which observed severe discipline, and made her do manual labour. He made her take care of a leper. Not even once did Devi Bahen fail. Travelling for miles, she went from place to place popularizing the message of Gandhiji by putting them into practice. She was a good organizer, a disciplined worker. People felt that the temptations of worldliness had not tainted her even one bit. Morning and evening, she used to hold on to the symbol of marriage tied firmly to a white string and pray. In Devi Bahen's opinion, a woman's soft emotions were a great sin. She would tolerate anger. But she never forgave

---

[43] A word coined by Gandhiji to refer to the lower castes. This literally means 'People of God', intended to make them feel equal to the upper castes.

lust. That was why she decided to do a remedial act till the end of her life for the mistake committed by a young woman whom she liked.

'During the Quit India Struggle, Devi Bahen was injured badly and wounded her forehead severely. Her right hand was smashed and hung loose. It was cured, to some extent, after many days of nature-cure therapy. Even so, the wound left a thick callus protruding from the forehead. During the pilgrimage to the Bengal region, Gandhiji used to say, "Look at Devi Bahen. The greatest symbol of fame is stamped on her forehead. It is because of that that I took her along with me during this journey."

'Thus, time passed. Gandhiji died. The Partition of India and the communal riots had altogether wearied many of us. The Swaraj which we desired for was not this. But, what else can an army without a leader do? From the front ranks, many of them dragged themselves upward, on to the seats of ministers and disappeared. Many became Members of Parliament. Some others became contractors and black marketeers, earned money and enjoyed life. In the country which practised prohibition, intoxicants began to flow through pipes. Untired by all this, Devi Bahen moved forward. She travelled for many days along with the yogi who moved on foot. She became involved in serving refugees. After that, she took over the work of Mahilashram. That was the time when the winds of pleasure-loving instincts had begun to affect even the inmates of the ashram. She introduced even stricter rules for the inmates. When a leader with a dubious reputation wanted to visit the ashram, she objected. She drew a comb, hair oil, and powder from the handbag of a member of the ashram governing committee and flung them away ...

'She was very harsh to several young people involved in social work. But, in the midst of all this, Devi Bahen had some peculiar weaknesses. She loved certain kinds of people. She utterly believed in the people whom she loved. She would even give her life for people she believed in.

'There was a refugee girl in the ashram from western Pakistan. A complexion of gold ... She was somewhat like you, Mrs Nair. Aquiline nose, long eyes and slightly coppery gold curly hair ... Devi Bahen named her "Thankam", and addressed her by that name. She said that that was the name she loved best. Thankam was as pure as milk, peaceful, and loving. During the prayer meetings, she sang sweetly. She participated in the social welfare activities. She worked very hard without wasting a single moment. She was Devi Bahen's constant companion. No one ever doubted her purity of character.

'It was during that time that a young man from the south joined the ashram. A young man of medium height, with ruddy complexion and curly hair. He claimed that he had long years of experience in the service of the country. He moved around in the villages and organized cultural meetings. He could sing, act, and speak very well. He used to direct and produce the plays he had written.

'Devi Bahen liked that young man. Did he resemble anyone whom she had known? In any case, she forgot herself so far as to send Thankam on tour as the heroine of the play, which the young man had organized for the upliftment of the villages. She would say, "It is not correct to disappoint sincere workers like Arun. If we had ten young men like him, our country would be saved. What an honest young man!"

'Even then, there were some murmurs that said Arun was a false name, and that he was someone's spy and a betrayer. But it was sinful to doubt a nice young man like him, whom everyone liked.' Kalyani Devi shook her head and continued—

'Today, I feel that what people said was true. After a long time, he who was the leader of the opposition party, a literary stalwart, and an important person had told me, "Kalyani Devi, I believed that the end would justify the means. If I had not lied the way I did to Devi Bahen, I would not have got refuge at that time. But, that wasn't my crime. I was an emotional person. Because of my weakness, I even spoilt that good woman's life."

'Yes, even when the police surrounded the ashram, searching for the revolutionary who was in hiding and discovered from Arun's bag banned literature and incendiary material, Devi Bahen was not shaken. She answered only the question about where they had hidden him, "We are Gandhiji's followers. Bappuji has told us that we should give refuge to seekers. I felt he was a nice man. He was also a good worker. Yesterday, he told me that he had to go to town on some important work and left, leaving his bag behind. I know nothing more."

'Believing in Devi Bahen's personal integrity, the police did not take any action in this case. Many of the Congress leaders knew her. The ashram merely received a severe warning that that there should be no repetition of such events ... But after this event, the work of the ashram suffered. Fear, suspicion, coldness. Many of the inmates began to leave. But it was not any of this that prompted Devi Bahen to take up sannyasam.

'The day-to-day work at the ashram was going on as usual. Prayer, spinning of yarn, weaving classes—all these activities continued in their routine fashion. For some days, Thankam had not been well at all. Headaches, vomiting, and fainting fits. Under the medical care of the village apothecary, she kept to her room.

'One day, early in the morning when Devi Bahen visited her, what did she see? Thankam sat squeezing the neck of a baby covered in blood. Her eyes were burning. She was gnashing her teeth. Her lips twisted outlandishly. Her expression at that time was of

Bhadrakali strangling Darika,[44] and sucking his blood. Devi Bahen looked at her just once, and began to tremble.

'In a husky voice, Thankam said, "Mataji, I am atoning for my crime. I erred. I am a sinner. I shall go. I shall correct my mistake through another mistake. I have seen my father and mother being strangled to death. My sister ... Oh ... I will not submit this child to such an experience. Let at least my baby attain moksha."

'After minutes of stony immobility, Devi Bahen said, "No, Thankam. You are not the one who made a mistake, it is I. I should have known better. I should have been careful. For all the mistakes that take place in this ashram, I alone must atone. Me alone. Doing penance for the rest of my life, I will wash away the stigma."

'Devi Bahen left the ashram. With this she began her self-torture. For many days, she fasted. She travelled to many places. Dipped in holy rivers. In the end, now they say, she is in the ashram of Suddhananda Saraswathi. She has herself become a goddess.'

Thinking of someone, bringing her palms together, and paying obeisance, Kalyani Devi walked out in a hurry. On that day, thinking of someone, how long did she, Thankam Nair, sit in meditation!

[44] This refers to the Puranic incident of Bhadrakali or Kali (mother goddess) killing the demon Darika.

Different Paths, Same Goals

All the images that fade in the piercing heat of the mid-noon sun receive a fresh coating of colour by the evening. Growth, if any, in old age can only be backwards. This became clear to her only when Devu grew up. Devu's childhood reminded Thankam Nair of her own childhood. Like all grandchildren, Devu drew very close to her grandmother. They did everything together: eating, sleeping, and bathing. After dinner, when she reached the bedroom, Devu would put her arms around Ammumma's neck, lean on her bosom and beg, 'Ammumma, tell me a story. Please. Just one story. I am not feeling sleepy.'

She did not like hearing a story more than once. When her stock of stories grew low, Mrs Nair began to recall stories from her own past. As she began to relate these very small events, which took the glow of imagination and the unusual beauty of actual experiences, Devu sat and listened, enthralled. The *utsavam* of Chengannat temple. How the elephant of the mana ran wild, gored its mahout and a few others, and came charging to the Kacheri Malika raising its call for the kill. The whole village of Chenagannat trembled. People scattered. There was not a man who had the courage to approach the elephant. When killing the elephant seemed inevitable, her father prayed to Chengannattappan and approached the elephant holding a bunch of bananas. 'Gangadhara!' he called just once. The elephant turned and looked at him. It lowered its forehead. Aphan Namboodiri placed the bunch of bananas in its extended trunk. More bananas were sent for and by the time all the bananas in Chengannattu village were used up, the trained mahout arrived and chained the elephant. 'Your grandfather was such a brave man.' How the crocodiles of Thonnippuzha used to strike both big and small boats with their tails, capsize them, and gobble the travellers in them. How the oracle in red silk and anklets carried the sword and ran around yelling '*Hiyyo, Hiyyo*' when there was a bout of smallpox in the village. Devu liked all these stories.

When she heard the story of how Unni Ettan sat swinging and twirling on the swing tied on the mango tree with her on his lap, Devu said, 'Ammumma! Do take me to your village. I must see Unni Ammavan. I too want to swing like you did.' She was only eight or ten at that time, but she was obstinate about getting what she wanted. That was how they went to the village.

Nair veedu had been partitioned. There were not many people there whom they could call relatives. But karmic bonds have always shaped the bonds of birth. They hold an unknown attraction. In father's illam, Aniyan Namboodiri ruled unchallenged. The insane younger aunt and the water-crazy grandmother had all died long ago. Aniyan talked of his new estate, this son-in-law's success and his plans for sending his son to England. There was a reception in modern style held in the new guest house. Everything was disciplined and orderly, adhering to the prevalent etiquette. Only when she asked where Unni Ettan was, he said, 'Ettan must be lying at the entrance to the temple and calling out to Chengannattappan for protection. Along with him there must be some riff-raff also. He is really mad. It is too late for any treatment.'

She remembered that Aniyettan had always been like this. Once before, when he had visited Delhi, he had said, 'I gave five thousand rupees to the war fund, Thankam!'

She made fun of him, 'Why? Could you not have given it to some poor people? You might have at least earned some virtue.'

'What do you know, Thankam! I will earn the title of Rao Bahadur. Unlike Unni Ettan, money for me is not to be used to earn virtue. It is pleasure that I seek to earn. To do so, you need to be a person of some significance.'

At that time, he was dressed in a gold-bordered shoulder cloth, silk shirt, and cap. A time of British rule.

She saw him next after India had won Independence and the Congress Ministry was in power. His apparel had changed dramatically. Coarse khaddar shirt, mundu, shawl. He had come straight to her house. As soon as he saw her, he said, 'Thankam, you are a lucky person. Husband in a good position! Children in good jobs! Your own house! You must have saved a lot of money. Yes?'

Continuing, he asked, 'Do you know why I have come to Delhi? Government has instituted rewards such as wages for suffering, copper plate, etc. Edathiamma is a person who has rebelled and fought a lot. Using her name and our family links, I must build a case that I too had been imprisoned for a long time. Wasn't your husband working in the Secretariat? If he can arrange something, it would be an honour in my old age!'

That was the sort of man Aniyettan was, she was not surprised. Stepping down carefully from the mana, she slowly made her way towards the temple. Her mind was throbbing. Her head was bowed. She felt a great feeling of guilt. This was a visit after a very long spell. What changes! The upper roof of the temple had again begun to decay. The branch of the banyan tree hung half broken. A temple which had once seen five pujas and three processions every day, there now was only the ritual of placing a washed banana leaf twice a day before the deity.

In the centre of the pandal for elephants, a lit brass lamp glowed. Surrounding it were many children and elderly people from the village. Before the brass lamp sat Unni Ettan reading the *Bhagavatham*. He looked emaciated. Graying tuft and sunken eyes, but, in a strange way, there was a happiness and a glow about him. Her Unni Ettan. Like a yogi immersed in *brahman*, Sree Sukabrahma Maharshi's[45] flow of verses reverberated in his pure and mellifluous voice.

'The good fortune of the people of Ambadi[46] is indeed surprising. Because it was none other than the complete brahman, the ultimate in bliss, who was their friend.'

Immersed in the constant intoxication of irrational bhakti, Unni Ettan's voice had become husky. His eyes overflowed. The listeners also wiped their eyes. It looked as though even the godhead Chengannattappan sat and listened, shedding tears of happiness. As she stood watching, her eyes and heart too began to brim over. She controlled her sorrow and called, 'Unni Etta!'

He turned and looked at her. He did not immediately recognize her. How time had flowed and how great the gap between them! When the sixteen-year-old sister, who had gone away, returns at sixty-five, holding her granddaughter by the hand, and calls out 'Unni Etta', it would surely be difficult for him to remember accurately. Is that not so, Unni Etta?

Oh! Those eyes widened. His lips parted in a silent gasp. His cheeks twitched. If there is an emotion that can be called happiness, then it was what Unni Ettan felt as he stumbled to his feet and approached her.

'Oh! Is this really you, Thankam, my young sister? *You* are here. Thankam you did not forget me!' He held her in a close embrace

---

[45] The sage who composed the sacred book, *Bhagavatham*, relating the story of Sree Krishna. Son of Veda Vyasa, the composer of Mahabharatam.
[46] The mythical city where Sree Krishna lived as a child.

and kissed her on her forehead. Time flew back fifty years, swinging on its axis. 'Devu, are you watching? Are you envious? Beloved daughter! This is your eldest uncle! Unni Ammavan! Fall at his feet and pay obeisance.'

Unni Ettan raised and held the girl who knelt and placed her head at his feet. He kissed her. He held her head lovingly on his chest. Then Mrs Nair remembered her childhood, when she had leaned her head on this same chest and fallen asleep.

'History is repeating itself, Unni Etta. She is my son's daughter, Devu. I am the one who named her. Devu! Devaki ... Are you pleased?'

For a minute, Ettan stood lost in some sacred memory. Then, caressing the child's forehead, he said, 'Very good, Thankam. An apt name. Isn't it the name of the great Sree Krishna's mother! A name all of us like very much! ... Then ...'

Ettan did not complete the sentence. But its meaning was complete. We did not say anything about Tethi Edathi. But the name that swelled in both their minds was hers. When she was about to return, she said, 'Come with me, Unni Etta! I have come here to take you with me. During our childhood, we were together. Our old age could also be spent together. We can go to Kasi, Haridwar, Rishikesh, and all other places. What if we can retrieve our lost days?'

Ettan shook his head, 'No, Thankam. No. I know that you love me. There is no one else who loves me as much. But my time is over. For a few meaningless beliefs, I pushed aside the good fortune of life. But I received one thing in exchange. The instinct to love this universe through God. Today, I realize that Man and God are one and the same. With that, I have retrieved everything I gave up. Why do I need pilgrimages? Or moksha? The Lord, who also is the universe, abides with me!'

Pausing a little, he asked, 'Thankam, did you see Aniyan?'

'Yes. There was a great reception also at the end of which he said, Ettan is mad and it is too late for treatment.'

'It is true, Thankam. I am insane. Giving up wealth, relatives, and everything that mattered, living in this dilapidated temple, if I am not a mad man, who is? But my madness is in bhakti. Aniyan's in wealth and power. For some others, it lies in serving the country. Will there be a generation without its own madness? Oh, God! Lover of devotees! Save me!'

Saying this, he picked up the offerings from the puja, puffed rice, jaggery, and a piece of coconut, and placed them in Devu's hands. 'Child, this is the only offering I can give you. Love, love God and Man. Love does not know separation. That is what the Lord says. May you be fortunate!'

As she returned, she felt very content. Unni Ettan had found the true purpose of life. Tethi Edathi was still searching for it. What about herself? Would she have the fortune to find true contentment?

Another meeting during that visit was also unforgettable. Puthusseri Kuttan Namboodiri, known as P.K.P., visited her at Nair veedu. He was the priest in one of the temples owned by Nair veedu. His son's son had passed the school's final examination. P.K.P. requested her help to find a job for the boy.

She sighed looking at that revolutionary whom she had once worshipped as a brave lover. He had turned into an old, thin, dark Brahmin, his back stooped with care and the disillusionments life had presented him with. His face bore marks from the many wounds received during the fight for justice. She felt very proud of the sister he had raised: a brave and unshakeable woman.

'Pension and medals of fame are presented to old freedom fighters as wages for sacrifices. You are a person who has suffered a great deal. Could you not have applied for one?'

He was as startled as though she had offered him an insult, and stood up, as though about to explode.

'Netyaramma, I did not come here as a beggar. I do not want anyone's charity. If I wanted wages for my sacrifices, could I not have accepted the gallows? The real wage for serving the country is that. Today, I am a poor man. I have four or five children and a family. Still, I work in whatever fashion I know best and earn a living. In labour, there is no distinction between "high" and "low". The real shame lies in selling one's ideals for money ... Do not expect me to do that ... I am going ... *namaskaram*! ...' His short, grey hair stood on end. His eyes blazed. Unable to control his anger, he rushed away. As she watched him, she felt that she had never loved any man so desperately.

'Ammumma! Is your head aching? Shall I apply some medicine on your forehead?' The touch of a very soft hand. So cool! Bliss! She lay enjoying it. The memories of old tragedies began to fade. Why be sad when she had such a sweet-natured granddaughter? The snow drops of sorrow after their hot slumber in the mind turn into pearls. Perhaps it was why the prayer beads of old age glowed the way they did. Mrs Nair held her granddaughter's palm and placed it on her eyes for a long while. After all, fate had entrusted the moksha of the older generation and the growth of the future one to these little hands. Isn't that why they had come to this place? Suddenly, as though remembering something, she asked, 'Devu, please check whether that bundle is still in Ammumma's bag. Please take care of it. It is a treasure.'

Treasure

Urukkidunnu mizhi neerilittu
Mukkunnu muttum bhuvanaikasilpi
Manushyahrittam Kanakatheyetho
Panittharathinnupayukthamakkan.[47]

The world's greatest craftsman
Melts gold—the human heart
Dips it in human tears, to shape it
Into a piece of work, unknown.

From somewhere beyond memory came flowing the lines of an old poem. Whose lines? Vallathol's? Ulloor's? Asan's? Nalappadan's?[48] In her youth, Thankam had read poetry keenly—Edathiamma's influence. Such a sweet voice! Whenever she came across good poems, she used to rush to Edathiamma with them, to make her recite them aloud. She enjoyed listening to them! Edathi herself used to secretly write poetry. Once, she had sent the following lines to her at college:

Dukhamallathe Mattonnumillenikkishta
Thozhiyayethorukalavumie

---

[47] This verse is taken from the long poem *Kannunirthulli* (Tear drop) by Nalappad Narayana Menon immediately after the loss of his wife.
[48] Famous twentieth-century poets of Kerala.

Ishtasodari! Neeyum Marannitho
Nashtabhagyayam Edathiammaye?

I have nothing now except sorrow
As my close companion
Dear sister! Have you also forgotten
This unlucky Edathiamma?

Was it like this? ... Or ...? ... Of late, her memory seemed unable to retain anything for long. A heavy weariness. Her arms hurt. Perhaps due to the injections. The after-effects of medicated sleep never quite faded. Dreams. Everything could be dreams. Life itself is a long dream. She could forgive herself for forgetting Edathiamma. But what about Unni Ettan? Unni Ettan, who had melted his heart, dipped it in his own tears, and forged it into pure gold. When her thoughts took this turn, she again became agitated. Reconnecting the broken links, the photographic images streamed through her mind. The curtain rose. The character of Ettan's mother appeared: a very proud woman who controlled and ruled the anthapuram. Aphan Namboodiri was merely the person who managed the family property. Inside the vast Manampalli mana, the people who came, left, or stayed—the comforts and welfare of all those people hung on the fingertips of Ettan's mother. She looked after matters concerning religious rituals. She ruled the servants. She behaved in an appropriate manner with each of her guests. The kitchen utensils, such as the big shallow vessel, the pans made of alloy materials, and the heavy frying pans, filled or emptied according to her commands. Even the mighty Aphan Namboodiri became humble when he entered the inner quarters. He had spoken to her only thrice and that too from the outer verandah.[49] They disagreed on three issues—first, Ettan's wedding; second, Aniyan's education; and the third on the remedial mea-

[49] The younger Namboodiri is not allowed to see his sister-in-law.

sure to be performed for Edathiamma. She had disliked Unni Ettan
marrying from Puthusseri illam. Her view was that the family
should look for a more beautiful girl from a wealthier and more
powerful house. But Aphan said, 'The horoscopes do not match.
There is chovva dosham in Unni's horoscope. He is destined to be
a sannyasi. Variar studied more than a hundred horoscopes. This
was the one which he somehow barely managed to match. The
astrologer is of the opinion that no match but this will take place.'

So, with a great deal of protest from Ettan's mother, Edathiamma's
wedding took place.

Aphan Namboodiri wanted to groom Aniyan to take his place
and oversee the tharawad matters and be trained to take charge
of the regional matters of Tiruvanthikkara.[50] There were a lot of
taxes coming from that region where the overseers were always
cheating them.

But Ettan's mother said, 'At my illam, my brother will not send
Aniyan to school without serious thought. Let him study. If you
don't mind, I think that would be best.'

In this matter, Aphan Namboodiri gave in, admitting defeat.
Aniyan was also supported by Netyaramma. Because of that,
Thankam also got some support.

On the third matter—atonement for Edathiamma—Aphan
Namboodiri was half-willing to bring her back. There was pressure
from Netyaramma also. Still, faced with the unending obstinacy
of Ettan's mother, he had to bow before her and give in. She said in
no uncertain terms, 'That useless woman ... She, who has given up
her umbrella and eats with untouchables not observing pollution
... That fallen woman will not be allowed to enter the gates of this
tharawad. If she enters, I will walk out through the other door.
There is no place here for both of us.'

[50] A region in Kerala.

Following this announcement, she began to relate the faults of Edathiamma to every visitor. Edathiamma was not beautiful. Her character was no good. She was barren. 'If that thing's[51] head shattered somehow, at least some good would have come to my Unni. Oh, Chengannattappan! Please make it happen! Please take care of the succession.' She even spread the rumour that Unni Ettan's second wedding had been fixed ... 'But, for that, we do need the permission of that first good-for-nothing woman. Only if she continues to stay away can the ritual take place. She has demolished this tharawad. Can't she go away somewhere? ...'

These rumours would have reached Edathiamma with ten-fold exaggerations. The Namboodiris always had people who claimed to be close to the family, who spread lies in return for a meal or for a length of old cloth. Edathi must have thought that she would stand aside to protect Unni Ettan's reputation. If you do not have a house, you can serve the country. You have to surrender your life for some cause or the other. That was probably why she went to Wardha. 'Let him worship his mother. I shall serve my Motherland. Both are after all similar.' She had heard that Edathiamma had sent a message to this effect.

But Unni Ettan spoiled all their calculations. A householder needed a wife to perform the rituals. He said that marrying beyond that was an *adharma*. Afterwards, without a word, he entered the book room or sat in the sanctum sanctorum of Chengannattappan ... For the first time in her life, in case of her obedient son, Ettan's mother had to admit failure.

When Thankam visited her village the previous time, it was Madhavi, Kunchi Varasyar's daughter, who told her all these stories. They were of the same age and had been classmates. This powerful matriarch suffered in the end from rheumatoid arthritis

[51] In the original, the reference to Edathiamma is *athinte* (neuter gender) to mark the matriarch's contempt and disregard.

and was bedridden for five to eight years. She died listening to many biting comments from Aniyan's wife. Madhavi said, 'She was that cruel a woman. She suffered for what she did. The way in which young Master Unni and the young mistress were subjected to mental pain, won't it bring its retribution?'

Thankam said nothing. Did Ettan's mother do all this thinking it was cruelty? Or had she thought of her son's and his tharawad's good fortune? Why was she, Thankam, thinking of all these things now? Even she had thought that Edathiamma had given up her husband for name, fame, and to fulfil an obstinate ambition. She had not thought of visiting the village even once to seek the truth. If she had, how different things would have been! Ettan, who had never denied Thankam anything, may have worn the mantrakodi and shoulder-cloth and clasped the henna-covered hands wearing the white ring, and once again gone through the installation ceremony. In her old age, that kind of a reunion would have given her great pleasure. But human history is dictated by time. It had already done all that it could have done.

Approximately two weeks earlier, she had received a letter and a parcel from her village. It was from Aniyettan. He had written:

Ettan has gone to his heaven. He was not doing well for a long time. But still, he would bathe, chant, and go to the temple. One day, he prostrated in the main mandapam of Chengannat temple and prayed, 'Grant me peace! Oh Lord! Grant me peace!'

When the priest went out and looked at him, there was no movement. Everything was over. I performed his death rites and the feast very grandly. In the Bhajanamadhom, there was a parcel addressed to you. I am sending it to you.

Yours, Aniyettan

She unwrapped the parcel; a bundle of old writing paper with a note:

For Thankam,

The only material wealth that I have, this parcel, I give to you, Thankam. This is very sacred. If you meet the owner, give it to her or leave it in the Ganga, or if you do not mind, give it to Devu in memory of this uncle. This is my last wish. My pindam lies in the hands of a woman. She sacrificed herself. See your daughter as my daughter. I will be fulfilled if I get a small ball of rice from Devu's tiny hands. My blessings are with her. If you meet the yogini, tell her I was always pleased with her. She has always been with me.

Your own Unni Ettan

She opened the bundle with curiosity. There was a cheruthali and *mani* strung on a white thread—Edathiamma's *mangalya-sutram.* She read the letter:

For your blessed feet,

We who were once far away have now drawn very close. I do not feel any separation at all. I can see, hear, and touch you. These many years, I have not slept without placing my head at your feet. Many a time have I wondered whether I should return. But, later, I felt Bhagirathi has fallen away from Himavan. No return is possible. Flow, flow, flow. If it is to the netherworlds, let this journey proceed that way. After wandering for many days, one thing is clear—however much we deny them, our relationships wrought through karma will always follow us. The flaws I thought I saw in you in those days, I now realize were virtues. That is where I too have arrived. When I got tired of life, I came out to serve society. Then, I turned to serving the nation. Having finished that too, I now wish to serve the ultimate truth. Who knows what is the truth, what is good? In any case, like in the path of birth, we have united in the path of work also. Now there is no separation. Once I had thought that I should give up my body and achieve moksha. But, even then, desires linger. Retaining these, will we be able to obtain release?

With Gurudevan's blessing, I am embarking on this experiment. Tomorrow I am going to assume sannyasam. Leaving this birth, I accept another. This object, which I always wore as the symbol of a karmic bond, I return to you. This was always my protection, my consolation, my armour. Grasping this, have I chanted the sacred names lakhs of times. As long as this was fastened tightly around my neck, I was courageous because I felt that I had a protector. But, today, at this decisive moment, before I give up any other bonds, I have to untie and remove this—this auspicious symbol of marriage purified by mantras. Please accept this and bless me. Henceforth, there is no Tethikutty. Only Sumitrananda. Greetings! ...

Your own ...

After reading that letter, how long had she sat unmoving? This small thali, which had broken the knot to which it was tied, frightened her like a serpent's hood. It burnt like glowing embers. At first, she had thought that she would throw it in the Ganga. But, by that time, that meeting—the real meeting had taken place—as though the goddess herself had appeared before her. At first, she was startled and speechless. Memories broke over her like waves. Like a book yet to be written, all the emotions came crowding in. Having seen everything, what peace! Real peace!

Mrs Nair sighed deeply, opened her eyes, and looked about her. She felt very relaxed. When she looked up, her son was standing next to her.

'Amme, you were very foolish. You are a chronic heart patient and weak. If you stand awake on the cold terrace, won't your illness intensify? Had I known this, I would not have brought you along with me.'

She laughed heartily, 'It doesn't matter, dear son! This mother is not the type who dies so easily. Were you very anxious?'

'What else? I heard the sound of something falling. Then a call. When I came running, you were on the floor. Immediately,

I picked you up and and laid you inside. Injection, medicine. Oh!
The struggle before you opened your eyes. Now, please, lie quietly.
You must rest.'

'I will lie down. But you must undertake to do something.
Before we return, you must take me to that yogini madhom. I will
find my peace only if I fall at that Mataji's feet. Will you make it
possible? Will you do that for me?'

'All right, I agree. I shall take you wherever you want to go. But
now be quiet and lie down. Sleep awhile.'

She smiled. Like a child obeying its mother, she pulled the covering over herself and turned on her side peacefully.

Whirlpools

Full moon in the month of Sraavan. Twilight. The sun was about to entrust his wondrous job to the moon and disappear. A light breeze. Over the Ganga, waves moved and tumbled like the desires of the human soul. As one disappeared, another rose, and then another. Generations. Eternal repetition. In the light which combined sunlight and moonlight, an ethereal peace spread. As a rule, on such days, Mataji of yogini madhom used to sit with her disciples singing sacred songs, while crowds thronged to listen. To them, a glimpse of Mataji was even more auspicious than a dip in the sacred river.

But, today, Mataji was deeply disturbed by an insulting question raised by some woman. She did not merely walk away. She ran as though she wished to escape from something—like trying to hide from someone—she ran so fast that the disciples could hardly keep pace with her. Four kathams. Eight kathams. Even if she had to cover a hundred *yojana*s, it looked as if she would have run at this speed. The shadow behind her lengthened. Finally, by the time she reached the courtyard of the yogini madhom, she was panting heavily. Even so, unmindful of her discomfort, she entered her meditation room, lit a lamp, and prostrated before it. 'Please give me the strength to endure anything … anything at all …'

Her senses broke loose. The *mandala* of her consciousness trembled. Mataji even thought that her very life was ending.

She felt exhausted.

A new experience for Mataji of yogini madhom.

Sumitranandayogini was a mendicant who observed severe penance and disciplines. For years, she had done solitary penance. She saw no human beings, looked at no one, spoke to no one. It was then that she met Swamiji. He tempered the heat of her hatred of the world. He transformed her into the gentle Mataji she was. 'There are many women in this world in greater agony than you. Embrace them. Try to console them. You will get peace.' She had paid heed to that advice and started to work. She gave shelter to many unfortunate women. People believed that any misfortune or illness could be cured by Mataji's touch. Admirers visited her the whole day. They brought flowers and fruits as offerings. They related their sorrows and sought consolation. For their sake, Mataji seemed to have forgotten herself and her needs. But today, after returning from the tirthaghat, she fell into a deep meditation. She did not have her usual meal of milk and fruits. She did not talk even to her closest disciples. She sat on the platform under the *vilva* tree behind the ashram. Vilva trees are not meant to be leant against. Their trunks are spiky. But their tender leaves spread a soft fragrance.

Somewhere on the slopes of the Sivalik range, smoke rose. Curling and twirling, the smoke rose to the abode of Vishnu.[52] It could be from some ashram. Or, from a factory. Or, it could be the last sacrifice of someone's life. Mataji tried consciously to reduce the weakness—of her own heart. A yogi's mind should be as immovable as that of a mountain. It should not be vulnerable like a river. But she also remembered with devotion that it was the moving Ganga which rushed to the netherworld and gave release to this world and the next.

[52] Lord Vishnu, second in the Hindu Trinity, responsible for the function of preservation in the cycle of life.

Close to the ashram, from some small hut, came the melodious singing of devotional hymns:

Gangatarangaramaniyajatakalapam
Gowrinirantaravibhushitavamabhagam
Narayanapriyamanangamadapaharam
Varanasipurapathim Bhaja Viswanatham.

His coiled locks made beautiful by the waves of Ganga,
His left side, constantly decorated by the presence of Gowri,
A favourite of Narayana, he sat,
The one who quenched the arrogance of Kama Deva
Pray to Viswanathan, who is the lord of Varanasi.

Who was reciting it? Who? From the abyss of the past, a well-known figure appeared clearly. A person seated cross-legged, at the time of *pradosha sandhya* after a bath and tying his damp tuft to the left side of his head. On his chest, a clean sacred thread. On his forehead, the mark of sacred ash. His eyes turned up in the heavenly intoxication of bhakti. In his pure and imposing voice the song continues:

Vachamagocharamanekagunaswarupam
Vagisavishnusurasevitapadapeedham
Vamena vigrahavarena kalatravantham.

That figure, which is the repository of all good virtues, which is unseen by eyes or unheard by words.
He, at whose feet, the god of words, Lord Vishnu, and other divine beings are seated;
On his left side his wife seated like an idol.

Oh! ... She thought she was going mad. The call of the previous life reverberated in every atom of her being. Thrice that evening she had denied, 'No ... No ... No ... a sannyasin has no past.'

But are human relationships such that they break off if you say no and reject them? During his last days Gurudevan used to say, 'Daughter, those who reject this world will be denied even the next world. The truth is the same in all the worlds. Life is the achievement through sacrifice. That is not hatred. Or disappointment. Or rejection. It is the state of a human being turning into a god. The call of the early life has reached me. I am going to my village now. Only after that can I seek to do the last rituals to attain nirvanam,' saying which he left.

He showered the nectar of his blessings on his relatives and devotees. But what about her? Who would be her support? Even before she took up sannyasam, there was no place to return to. Husband, brother, family. After losing everything, she had entered the forest. Even after a long life of sannyasam, she did not feel like facing those who had called themselves her relatives. Abandoning everything, she had pushed herself into the mouth of death. How many times had she tried to commit suicide? Still she did not die. She felt that it was not the fear of sin, but the accidental nature of the event that had always saved her.

Mataji raised her hand to her forehead to touch the area where the wound had not healed completely and caressed the callus of the big wound on her forehead.

Ha! At that time she wanted to die as a martyr ... It was not fulfilled. Coming to think of it, which of her desires had been fulfilled?

She had wanted to uplift society. To uplift the country. She wanted to build a new world filled with firm ideals. What had happened? Was it because of the mistake of an inmate that she had given up the world? Or was it a remedy for the results ricocheting from her own deeds? Her mind was restless. There was anger, sorrow, and helplessness. She wanted to discard everything. There was only one thing she had on hand to throw and break.

Her crushed and broken life! Picking it up, she had wandered to this sacred place. If she did die, let it be here. For seven days and nights she had wandered in the dirty side streets where cows, dogs, horses, donkeys, women, children, and old men rubbed shoulders and moved around. She had bathed in the sixty-four bathing ghats and tried to wash away her sins. (What was her sin?) She had paid obeisance to the 1,008 idols of Shiva. She prayed without food and sleep. Still she did not get peace. At last, on the eve of a midnight, while she stood in knee-deep water in Kedar ghat, she fell into thinking. In the river which flowed fast, the stars of the sky were mirrored as moving images. The really magnificent figure of universal nature! She stood there for a long time bringing her palms together. She had not decided to die. Still her legs went deeper and deeper into the water. She stepped deeper and deeper into the river. The water touched her waist and then reached her breasts.

Then who stopped her holding on to her shoulders? Lord Shiva? ... Fate? ... Her guru? ...

On that day, her guru told her that since she had not visualized and created human life, she did not have the right to destroy it either.

'Is there a state when you yourself become not your own?'

'Yes, daughter, I will teach you about that.'

So she came away. She walked and walked this far and had reached here. Having fallen at the feet of her guru, she had forgotten all her sorrows. But today ...? In the end, she had failed. She ran away from the presence of love. She desired strongly to find the woman she had met in the morning and embrace her. That woman would have given her love and peace. She would have given her everything which she had searched for so far ...

'What is this love which has been praised so much?' she thought. In one sense, wasn't even that selfishness? An illusion? A disorientation of the mind? This was a doubt she herself had raised with several seers. Many people had put this question to her too. A sannyasi, who has to give up all emotions, does he have to bear the burden of this individual relationship? In the *Upanishad*, Yagnyavalkya[53] tells his wife, 'Maitreyi, a wife loves herself for her own sake. The husband who loves the wife also does it for the happiness of his soul. No one really loves anyone except themselves.'

Suddenly, from somewhere from the depths of days gone by, she heard another resounding answer. Years back, maybe in Krita yuga another husband told his wife, 'Love is not an emotion, Tethikutty. It is a kind of behaviour, an experience, a kind of merging. Those who do not understand this, will never gain true happiness.'

Yogini Mother was startled. Who had said this? When? Where? Was it in this birth or in the previous one?

However much she tried to control herself, she fell headlong into a tornado of memories.

A self-contained bedroom, on the southern end of the western section of the building. Moonlight crept in through the small windows and lay scattered. In the wind, a whiff of the fragrance of jasmine and *pavizhamalli* ... The clear brilliance of the brass lamp. Seated on the grass mat spread on the floor a young woman waits for her husband. Every footstep on the staircase thrilled her. Why had she entered such a big tharawad? Why did she get such a good husband? They were bound by shackles of duties. She thought that she would have had a better life with a poorer man, a practical and lustful man. He might beat her. Ignore her. But

---

[53] A great sage and preceptor to King Janaka; Maitreyi was his wife. A section of *Brihadavangaka Upanishad* comprises a conversation they have on the absolute self.

at least sometimes he would caress her tenderly. When she read aloud Vallathol's poems, this man, her husband, quoted from the *Bhagavad Gita* and wearied her.

On such a night, when he came upstairs very late, he said, 'Tethikutty, you must be getting bored waiting for me. What can I do? By the time the religious rituals end, the overseers arrive with their accounts. Aphan comes to advise me. As for me, I can't understand a word of what he says. Yet don't I have to do my duty? Tethikutty, if you feel sleepy, don't wait for me.'

The young woman would complain tearfully, 'This duty that you talk about, has the *Gita* said that you have no duty to your wife? Aphan and his assistants have many other people. But for me, who is there in this birth except you?'

The young man would stroke her back and console her, 'You and I are one, Tethikutty! We may not be able to sit together all the time. But, we are one. If you realize that, you won't be sad.'

That young woman had not realized this fact, and the way she had suffered greatly was something that Mataji now remembered. A wick of light, which had fallen from her revolutionary brother, burnt in her mind. Obstinacy. Pride. Self-pride. Great expectations. She yearned for the release of not only herself, but that of her society and her country. She had hundreds of complaints about her life—her freedom—and even her way of dressing. She protested vehemently. She ardently desired a change. Whenever she mentioned that, he would stroke her shoulders and console her, 'It is not yet time, child! It is not yet time. The controller of time, the great Lord of the universe, will show the way for everything. Wait for that.'

But time was waiting for both of them. Time called. She left. Did he know where she had finally reached?

Breaking all the dams, tears began to flow from Mataji's eyes. They flowed and flowed and fell. Again they welled. She did not bother to wipe them. The unmoveable Sumitranandayogini, let her be an ordinary woman for at least one day, today.

When the steel wires, which had tightened the knot of her mind loosened, there was something she understood. No one is ever completely free. The bondage of custom. The bondage of law. The bondage of desire. Even the bond of love feels like a shackle. the Does the pitiable human soul ever get a release from this?

Who had said so once? She did not remember. Was it Arun? Or the strong sardarji in the Delhi police station with reddened eyes? While he stood in the midst of many young women, he was about to crack a crude joke. Suddenly, glancing at her face, he fell silent and froze. He said, 'I am unable to say it because Devi Bahen is here. On her forehead is the mark of a goddess. No one who looks at her can harbour a bad emotion.'

What is a bad emotion? He did not say. Was it lust? Was she a woman born to conquer lust? Who knows? She searched the depths of her inner mind. That day, in the bedroom, was it the dissatisfaction that she had felt about sex that led her through another path? In the end, she had won over that emotion. She hated it. Discarded it. Even the word *kaamam* used to make her furious. But was she able to hate that desire to create, which lay hidden in every living being? With a sigh she looked around the surroundings of the ashram—disciples, children. Amme. Mataji. Yes, for a woman any desire of life ultimately finds salvation only if it reaches this ghat. 'My children!' she wanted to call out and kiss all the beings of the universe. But no one wants a mother. They want only a guru. A yogini. Worship is what they needed ... Ha ... If only she could see one child who called out to her with a full-heart 'Amme' ...

The dawn was bursting open. Ganga woke up. Morning hymns filled the air. Yogini Mata became aware of her surroundings. After many days, she had forgotten her daily routine, and even herself.

Immersed in sinful thoughts not befitting a sannyasin, she had broken discipline and control.

Mataji stepped hurriedly into the Ganga and immersed herself. Without wiping herself dry, she ran. She prostrated in front of the picture of her guru kept on the prayer platform. 'Release me, Gurudevan! Release me! I can't bear it any longer. I am tired. Please accept me.'

Wonder of wonders! It was not the guru's face that appeared in front of her, but the face of another gentle *yogeeswara* ... Had it always been with her? Was he her gurudevan? Pressing her forehead on the floor firmly, she mourned, 'No. I have no liberation from you. You are my God. Guru. Leader. Forgive me, Gurudevan! Accept this sinner. At that time you used to say, love knows no separation. You have never been separated from me. What greater good fortune for me than to meditate on you.'

That whole day, the Yogini Devi lay prostrate on the bare ground. 'The Bhoomi which tolerates everything, which bears so many things. There are black snakes, hard rocks; aeons of human generations' cultures and mortal remains. The voice of yugas sleeps here. Green outwardly, inside a burning fire. Sita![54] Mother of human beings! You sought protection there. Please accept me also. Please give me a place at your footstool.'

On that day, Mataji ate nothing. Nor spoke to any one. By the time people assembled for the twilight worship, she had regained her balance. No one had seen Amma so peaceful, charismatic, or glowing before. On the *darbha* grass mat, she sat with her legs crossed. People came, prostrated, and sought advice from her. No one ever knew that a while before she had been an ordinary woman, who had dwelt on human emotions and wept for them. When the prayer meeting ended, Yogini Devi told her disciples,

[54] The epic Ramayanam's heroine and Lord Sree Rama's wife.

'Tomorrow onwards, I will be observing penance. I will take only water filled in a conch shell with three basil leaves in it; I will meditate in silence. Only after twelve days will there be a prayer meeting. I am doing this as an expiation for a sin.'

A Face in the Flames

There are many sannyasis, *sidhas*, and yoginis in the northern parts of India. Some walk naked in dangerous forests and live freely as forest animals do. Others meditate on the slopes of snowy mountains, in caves or under trees, and do severe penance. There are others who established *gurukulas* like the ancient hermitages of sages, did penance, and taught disciples. Some established modern hospitals and colleges and, thus, served the world. There were 'guru maharajas,' who flew their own planes and travelled the world to popularize yoga. This was the centre of India's spirituality. Those who were anxious to learn could approach the kind of gurus who suited them. They could share their doubts, become disciples. The nerve systems of religion are situated in the summits of the Himalaya.

But Sumitranandayogini's small hut was quite different. It stood modestly in a village four kathams away from the tirthaghat, where the city's low-level officers, sweepers, and workers lived. She had not been here for a long time. For many days, she had sat exposed to severe cold and sunlight, meditating under the trees. The villagers assembled and supplied her with some milk or fruits. Gradually, when people began to believe in her, they built a small hut for her. Women and children approached her saying 'Mataji, Mataji'. Every evening Amma would read from the epics. If anyone asked, she would explain the meaning to them. She would relate short stories which were closely related to real life. She did not pretend that she was a superior being. The ignorant villagers considered her to be a goddess. Here is a true yogini. She knows everything. The belief that her blessings would never fail grew and spread. Most of the intellectuals who visited the tirthaghat made it a point to come to the yogini madhom and talk to Mataji. A unique experience. Every day, she would not only recite verses from the *Gita* and the *Upanishads*, but also sing the long beautiful poem *Narayaneeyam*.[55] Sumitrananda's reputation as a yogini filled with knowledge, detachment, and love spread. She never said a single word about herself. But the people discovered that this disciple of Suddhananda Saraswathi bore the stamp of a social worker and satyagraha practitioner. They discovered that she was a Brahmin woman from the southern parts, born to the tradition of Sree Sankara. Mataji dressed only in khaddar. Every day, for an hour, she used to sit at the *charka*, spinning. Mother advised the village women, 'You must make what you need. So Bhagavan has ordered. We must clean our minds, bodies, houses, and country. Bhagavan will linger only in clean places.' She achieved through these words the kind of changes that a thousand social workers could not. 'Where there is mother, there is God also,' is what people believed.

In the meditation room of the yogini madhom burnt a fire which was never put out. Sannyasins had no need to perform sacrifices. Still, only after giving a portion of what she received to the fire, would she eat. 'Oh, Agni! This is for you, not for me.'

---

[55] A sacred poem comprising a hundred chapters, describing the story of Lord Narayana. It consists of 1,036 slokas and is a condensed version of the *Bhagavad Purana*. It is supposed to have been composed by Meppathur Narayana Bhattathiri, in the precincts of the Guruvayoor temple where he lay, seeking to be cured of his acute rheumatism.

When the ghee, milk, and cooked rice lay burning in the fire, it spread a fragrance which was like that of a Namboodiri illam, half a century back. 'Fire is life,' she would explain to devotees. 'Fire accepts the rice for the entire human race. He is called Vaiswanaran,[56] the universal man. Life-giving fire.'

When she closed her eyes in meditation, she would recall a face seen first in the glow of a thousand burning wicks. On the wooden plank, before the sacrificial fire was seated the wedded pair. The husband held the sacrificial objects close to his heart and whispered, 'Oh Agni, Prajapathi,[57] this is yours, not mine.' After the sacrifice, he turns around and decorates the forehead of his waiting bride. Thrilling moments. In those days, she had felt that life and sacrifice were one and the same. Even now, she, an old woman, a renunciate, did not consider this thought sinful.

Once a visitor asked, 'Mother, why are you burning a fire even at the height of summer? Throwing into the fire food which is meant to appease human hunger?'

He was a famous physicist. Mataji said, 'I do not know anything about science. Nor do I know how to argue. I just do what my heart says is right ... Take this too as a superstition. I think that a portion of my food should be surrendered to the Life of the Universe. Agni is the symbol of hunger. Pure imagination. But it satisfies me.'

Only one half of what the Yogini Mata said was true. Her inner soul said that she conducted this sacrifice bearing in mind someone for whom she should have cooked, someone she should have served. Before he ate, that man used to invoke the divine beings of the universe and offer rice. He used to say that even the worms and flies were included in this ritual. Though she had given up all worldly relationships, Mataji continued this ritual as she was

[56] The God of Fire.
[57] Brahma or Sun God, the king of the devas.

unable to control her inner being. Therefore, she used to perform this sacrifice without fail. Whenever there was a discussion on Fire, she remembered this story from Greek mythology heard long ago in Calcutta. The date was 15 August 1947. Independence Day. In a small hut in Kalighat, a sorrowing old man and his followers were resting. The town was lit up decoratively. The country forgot everything and rejoiced in its freedom. Cheers of victory rose to the sky and there were flags and festoons all around. Speeches. Processions. Isolating himself from all these, the disappointed leader sat cross-legged on a grass mat, immersed in his own thoughts. The charka was spinning. The rhythmic chants of Rama's name. For a long time, no one said anything. Then ...

'Why did you not go to Delhi? Is it not a victory after a tortuous war? You are the leader. Aren't victorious cheers raised everywhere in your name?'

For some time, he said nothing. He continued to stare at the white yarn emerging from the charka. In between, he joined the broken ends and said, '"Freedom?" Freedom! That is right. Let it come and be celebrated. But this is not my idea of freedom. My freedom is not one to be celebrated standing in partitioned India—surrounded by the hellish scenes of blood, tears, fire, and smoke. I did not fight for this or pray for this. Children, I am a failure, a thoroughly defeated man! Please leave me alone. Reject me! Isolate me!'

When she heard these heartbreaking words, she remembered an experience she had had a few days before. It happened during a tour. They were walking silently through a village, which bore the stamp of burnt houses, smashed bodies, raped women, and orphaned children. The only sound heard was the one that came from the leader's walking stick when it hit the ground. It was twilight and desolate. Suddenly, he turned round and asked, 'Devi Bahen, can you see the path ahead?'

'Yes, Bappuji!'

'It is getting darker,' he warned. 'Take care when you walk. You should not slip and fall.'

After that, he asked his followers to sing his usual marching song, composed by Rabindranath Tagore.

'If they are not following you—Oh unlucky one! Go on alone ...' the song which began like that. The poet accompanying them sang it in a heart-rending manner. It ended—

Pathirappekkattil Ghorandhakarathil
Deepamuyarthuvanalillenkil
Vedanayamiditthiyilabhagaha! Nin
Chetana Kathijjwlichidatte.
Aa velichathil kulichuninneedatte
Bhumiyum, Swargavumakamanam.

In the maddening storm brewing in the dawn,
In the terrible darkness.
If there is no one to raise the lamp
In the thunderous fire of your pain, Oh, unfortunate one!
Let your consciousness blaze and shine.
And let earth and heaven be bathed in that light.

When it reached that point, they felt as though a comet was blazing in front of them. Is there no one to blaze that fire today? To light a wick and show the path?

Thus immersed in old memories, suddenly, the lights went out. The sound of stone throwing all around. An attack. It was in the midst of this confusion that an old man, whose name she did not know, asked her, 'Bahenji, do you know how Fire came to this earth?'

She could have answered that it was one of the five elements and that it reigned in the hearts of all human beings. But what she said was 'No, I don't know.'

'There is an old legend about it, a story from Greek mythology. In the olden days, fire belonged exclusively to the gods in the Heavens. Light, warmth, and development were possible only for the devas. The earth lay frozen in the cold. In the dark space of earth, human beings shivered, crawling around like retarded beings. Prometheus, a deva, could not bear to watch this sad sight. Unknown to any of the inhabitants of heaven, he blew a spark of fire onto the earth. Even though it was a mere spark, that was all it needed to burst into a blaze. Spreading from one to another, the fire lit ovens and lamps to shine all over the earth. Man became strong. Man acquired intelligence and light. The image of the face of the earth itself changed. Only in the end did the devas understand this truth. With their special insight, they located the culprit. Prometheus accepted the charge humbly. The devas punished him for the crime of having given fire to man. He was chained to a rocky terrain between two great oceans. Every day, a vulture flew down and pecked and tore out Prometheus's kind heart and ate it up. Every night, the torn heart mended and regained its former state. And the next day, the vulture would again arrive to tear and pluck, with its cruel talons, his heart and eat it. Again, that night his heart would restore itself. Thus, the vulture tearing up his heart and the recreation of his heart happened continuously. Why did the heart keep regenerating every night for the vulture to tear and eat? Or, why was the vulture not sated after so many attacks? Even now, on another day, the deva may appear and ask, "Prometheus, if you get fire once again, would you still give it to Man? Would you make the earth equal to the heavens?"

'What would Prometheus answer? "Oh, Deva! So far you have not been able to put out the fire in my heart. That fire is for man. Imparting warmth to the frozen human being, this heart has grown steadily—a fire which is for giving—to blaze that fire, I am very happy. Earlier, I had only one heart. Today, I have a generation of eternal new hearts. Like flowers that bloom every day, a series of new hearts. Oh, Deva! Please send the vulture again and again. Chain me once again. This fire, which blazes on account of the act of giving to others, let it never die."

'We do not know what the Deva said on hearing Prometheus's words. But, Bahenji, even today there are vultures ready to tear apart people in whose hearts fires blaze.'

Having said these words, that nameless person walked through the crowds of violent people shouting ugly slogans and disappeared into the darkness.

Anything to do with fire—lamp, glow, flame, warmth—intoxicated her. Suddenly, in her mind's screen, a clear picture appeared. Mataji remembered.

Somewhere in the mists of past time, a river flowed. A huge cargo boat in that river. Travellers who had covered themselves. In the midst of these travellers, a ten-year-old girl. She was looking out. What sights! Water flowers, herons, crocodiles. Above, in the clear blue sky, the crescent moon taking its form. *Hai!* How beautiful! After a long way, the river divided into two streams. It was taking a turn. On the shores, a building which reached up like a flagstaff. Many burning candles. The peal of bells! The song which began 'O Mother, filled with goodness ...' The girl called her brother and said, 'Elder brother! Here is a temple. Shall we get down and pray?'

'That is not a temple. It is a church, the Christians' place of worship. Why, child, do you want to get down here and pray?'

'Yes, I do want to,' replied the child. At that time, she had believed that worshipping in any temple where the lamp was lit was an auspicious act. The only elder brother of an only sister. He would fulfil any whim of hers. Pulling the boat near the shore, the young man held the girl's hand and walked. They climbed the steps to the church. The figure of Jesus Christ crucified on a cross.

Near him was his mother, holding the child Christ. All around lit candles burning, the kneeling people rising and praying, 'O Mother, filled with goodness! May our prayers be with you! May our prayers be with you! Like in the heavens, may it come to the earth also ... Amen!'

'Who is that mother?' asked the girl. 'Is she the mother of Sree Krishna or Sree Rama?'

'No, child, it is a statue of Mariyam, the mother of Jesus Christ. There has been no mother as lucky as her. She had a son, who sacrificed himself for the welfare of the human race. All right, let us go. Mother should not know about this. She will scold us.'

They went down the steps. The child could not understand anything her brother had said. Still she thought, 'Ah! What a nice mother. What dignity. I too want to be a mother like her.'

The mother who sat under the covered portion of the boat was on her way to Guruvayoor for a ceremony of worship. A young widow. Devotee. A person who had strong ideas on pollution and non-pollution. When she heard what had happened, she scolded, 'To make a child step inside a Christian church. Kuttan, you are mad. Make her take a bath and change her clothes. You too must take a bath. After that recite the *Panchakshara* 1,008 times.'

That day, they had obeyed their mother. But that was the day on which the image of a mother was strongly imprinted in her imagination. She desired motherhood greatly. But, it had never been possible for her. Did Thankam have a son? If she did, what did he look like? The Yogini Mata began to tremble. The mind, as wild as a monkey in the forest, refused to stay under control. Even when she was meditating on the ultimate God, it obstructed her. Suddhananda Swami had said during his last days, 'Daughter! I know that your mind has not yet reached a state of peace. You are restless. You have not been freed from your earlier desires. But there is a fire glowing in your heart, a pure sacrificial fire. Place yourself in it and burning yourself, purify your life. See the man as God and worship him. Serve him. Every human being is a God. *Tat Twam Asi*—Thou art that. Know this and experience it.'

Gurudevan placed his palms on her head and blessed her, giving her a rare vision. The oceans of the entire living earth became one and appeared in front of her. Innumerable blazing planets. Several suns and moons. People. From worms to ants every being covered with the same glow. Like Arjuna's[58] *Viswaroopadarsanam*, for a moment, she stood stunned. Then she became conscious. She prostrated at her guru's feet and said, 'Gurudevan, I feel blessed, very blessed. Please bless me always.'

Thus, she had carried this undying fire and stepped out to serve God by serving man. She wiped the tears of the sorrowing. Smiled at children. She became pure, immersing herself in the plays of human beings in their universal nature, and worshipping the primordial spirit. But still, desires followed her. The mind vacillated. Control. Rules. Penanace. Mataji sat before the sacrificial fire, gathered the strength of the five elements, and tried to strengthen herself. She repeated to herself, '*Om Namo Narayanaya.*'

On the banks of the Ganga, a priest was reading the Ramayanam and explaining it. Hanuman[59] had completed the burning of Lanka. It was the section where he lamented whether he had accidentally burnt Sita also. Then he consoled himself:

Adhava, Charusarvangi
Rakshita swena tejasa

[58] The third Pandava prince and great warrior in the Mahabharatam who granted a glimpse of the true power of Bhagavan Sree Krishna.

[59] The monkey-hero of the epic Ramayanam, lieutenant and advisor of Sugreeva, and an ardent devotee of Rama.

Na Nasishyathi Kalyani
Naagniragnow Pravarthate.

Tapasa Satyavakyena
Ananyathacha Bharthari
Api sa nirddahedagnim
Na Tamagni Pradhakshyathi.[60]

Or otherwise that utterly beautiful one
Has been saved by her own glow
That pure woman will not perish
Fire has no effect on another fire.

With her penance, honesty, and faithfulness
She might burn the fire,
But, no fire can burn her.

---

[60] Verses 22 and 25, respectively, taken from Valmiki Ramayanam, *Sundara Kandam*, 55th chapter. Translated from Sanskrit to Malayalam by Vallathol Narayana Menon.

Hail, a New Yuga

The dawn of the twelfth day in the month of Sraavan. Today, Mataji will complete her fast and eat something. Today, ends the penance. Once again, that pure sweet voice will ring. The questions and doubts of the devotees will be answered. The mother of the villagers would wake again. Very early in the morning, a crowd had begun to gather in the yogini madhom. Everyone was nervous. An elderly woman hermit performing the difficult penance to eradicate sin. Why? In Mataji's case, there could be no sin at all. She, Suddhananda Saraswathi's disciple, what could her crime be for the performance of such an atonement? If not for the welfare of the world, why should a sannyasin do penance? Perhaps it was the first step in the final stage before nirvanam. It was said that even Suddhananda Saraswathi had blessed his disciples, entered a cave, and attained *samadhi* on the seventh day. The disciples waited anxiously, fearfully, and devoutly. They offered gifts. There were hushed whispers.

'No. Nothing will happen to Mother. Her blessed self had once fasted for forty-one days, like Gandhiji. Through his penance, he would atone for the errors his disciples made. Mataji was, after all, Gandhiji's disciple. Oh God! Save her from danger.'

'Mother might be praying for us. Even after such intense advice, we have not changed. What sins are committed in the tirthaghat? Even sannyasis have turned sinners. The power of the universal spirit of illusion alone can destroy it. And she is a yogini!'

'It seems that once in tirthaghat, a woman tested her and poked fun at her. From that moment, she fell silent. On that day when she returned to the ashram, she meditated the whole night. She began this penance the next day ... Devi! *Mahamaye!* Please forgive us! Please bless us!' prayed a woman devotee, her eyes filled with fear.

The Yogini Mata heard none of this. She meditated, merging with her inner self. Occasionally she opened her eyes, accepted gifts from disciples, and after consigning a portion to the fire handed over the remaining to her disciples to be distributed. The fire, fed with milk, ghee, and rice glowed with a primeval power. The yogini shone brighter than the fire itself. Her body, which after penance and fasts had grown frail, glowed like a golden arrow. She sat cross-legged in the *padmasana*. Lips clamped. Eyes half opened. An otherworldly peace, Not like Parvathy in the hermitage, but like Sita in Valmiki's[61] ashram. A magnificent image!

At the time of the Prasanna puja, the women disciples rang the bell and woke up Mataji. The milk and the sanctified water with which she broke her fast was covered and placed by the pit where the sacred fire was lit. But she did not notice it at all. She was busy blessing and receiving the salutations offered by devotees who streamed in. The devotees were not thinking of the mother, but only of her blessing. They pushed and crowded around as if to say, 'Me first, me first!'

When the crowds dwindled, Mataji raised her head and looked up. Her benign eyes swept the crowd and caressed them. Long, thick, graying eyebrows—between them, eyes filled with gentle, beautiful sympathy. In the middle of her forehead, a mark from a scar larger than the callus, due to frequent prostration.

[61] The sage-poet, who composed the Ramayanam, famed as the first poet of India.

Suddenly, she saw a woman seated far behind the others, sliding into a faint, murmuring as she collapsed, 'Oh my Edathiamma ... my ... my ...'

As the whole audience sat stunned and continued to stare, Yogini Mata rose slowly and came forward. She caressed the forehead of the devotee. 'Oh, pure one! Be comforted. May the ultimate being protect you.'

The fair, stout woman with snow-white hair, who wore pure white clothes, placed her head in the lap of a beautiful, sobbing young girl who resembled someone Yogini Mata had once seen and now forgotten. The dignified man who stood by her said, 'Don't worry. This happens often and will pass soon.'

Yogini Mata went on chanting. Sensing her touch, the old woman opened her eyes. They looked at each other for a long time, utterly still. Then, holding Amma's hand stretched towards her, the elderly woman sat up slowly. She brought her palms together prayerfully and fell on her knees. Her eyes filled with tears. Stuttering, she said, 'Please forgive me, Amme! I have come to you again. I could not help it. Please forgive my folly. In distant Kerala, I had a guru. A teacher, a holy man. He blessed me saying that some time I would meet with my Goddess, and accept offerings from Her. He said to me, "At that time, please offer my blessings also. And tell Her, I was always pleased with her. Always. Always."'

Mataji asked in an unemotional voice, 'Where is that guru now?'

The admirer's throat quivered, 'He is not alive now, Amme! He did not belong to this world. He went back to the world he came from, and before departing said, My successor is a woman. Your daughter is the continuation of that line. She is named Devaki. "Oh, Devakiputra,[62] please protect me!" It seems he died crying aloud these words.'

---

[62] Devaki's son, Sree Krishna.

Sumitranandayogini did not tremble. She did not turn pale. Nor did she faint. 'How long have I been begging for this kind of a release. Why am I not granted that?' Appearing to be voicing this question, stunned, she sat for a moment gazing at the sky, after which she said slowly, 'Those who departed are the lucky ones. The ones who remain behind are to be pitied. You know this, don't you? Oh, pure woman! Why do you follow me who has given up all worldly desires? What do you desire?'

The admirer burst into tears this time. She said, 'I did not embark on a pilgrimage at this age without a purpose. I have sinned many times. I forgot people dear to me. I was steeped in worldly pleasures. Wealth and position made me haughty. Besides all that, I am a sinner who broke the promises I made. In my youth, I had a friend. Not just a friend. A relative. Not just a relative, but one dearer than life itself! I had given her my word that my children would be hers too. That I would never, not even once, forget her. Then I forgot myself in the intoxication of worldly joys ... forgot everything. This journey is an atonement for that sin. Fortunately, I met you. You know everything. You are a goddess. Just utter the word, I am forgiven! Accept these children! Bless us!'

'There is no such thing as sin, pure woman!' Yogini Mata said. 'Who forgives whom? Who has not sinned? What is sin? When we reach the presence of the ultimate God, there will be no difference between sin and good deeds, or between pleasure and pain. Even the future and the past will fuse. What remains is only the ultimate truth: the truth of love. Understand this; gain peace of mind.'

The elderly devotee sat for a while, sunk in her thoughts. Then she opened her handbag and took out a small bundle. 'This is the gift my guru gave our child. It is marked by the sad story of an auspicious marriage. Touch it with your sacred hands, bless it, and give it back or reject it! Without your touch, it has no sanctity or purity.'

Yogini Mata opened the bundle unemotionally. She took out a small thali, fastened to a shabby white thread. For a minute, she looked at it carefully. After that, without any visible emotion, she offered it to the fire in front of her saying, 'This belongs to the fire, not to me.'

The string burnt down like the rust of materiality. The gold caught fire and glistened softly. Unhesitatingly, Yogini Mata took out that burning metal with her long, slim, bare, wrinkled fingers. She cooled it with pure water, from the vessel with the spout, placed it between her palms, and rubbed it till it shone. Then she placed the shining metal in the hands of the girl as beautiful as the dawn and as pure as the flowers used for worship, saying, 'Child! This is for you. This is pure gold! Do not mix it with anything inferior. Melt it and make something your generation likes. A word of caution. Never seek to change its radiance and purity. May you be happy.'

Yogini Mataji raised her eyes skyward. It looked as though she was watching someone somewhere. Like giving shape to the ultimate and making it real. As though merging with the ultimate. No pain here, no sorrow, no desire, no disappointment. She felt only the endless satisfaction of the soul. The world seemed to be in a trance. She looked like a deva, her wings outspread, ready to fly.

At that moment, when movement seemed impossible, quite suddenly, the crowd saw the man who stood behind the elderly disciple moving forward and falling at Mataji's feet. He said nothing, but his eyes filled. 'Amme! Come back! Come back! Come back,' he begged her. 'Here I am, finally I have come here. I have come. I have ...' He broke down.

Mataji withdrew her eyes from the sky above. Below, before her, his head on her feet, her son. Her son, not a disciple, not an admirer. Her real son. For a moment she hesitated. Then, placing her palms on his head, she ruffled his curling grey hair. Blessing or acceptance? On her sobbing lips, a silent cry.

'Son ... My son!'

Unborn generations must have heard this cry.

'Mother!'

'Son!'

'Mother!'

'Son!'

All beings moving and unmoving must have repeated this call. It must have resonated till eternity. Breast milk seemed to ooze from all of Nature. The end of penance—a new age being born. Even the blessing was wordless, 'May you be happy. Happy! ... Happy!'

Taming the Fire

On Adapting *Agnisakshi*[1]

Lalithambika Antharjanam's *Agniskashi* (1976) is an important literary text in Malayalam for the manner in which it writes the woman back into Kerala's reform project, not only in terms of women's roles and agency in the movement, but also in highlighting their high stakes in it. It also enriches our understanding of Kerala's experience of modernity, not solely as a tryst with tradition that yielded linear narratives of history and development, but as a more complicated, complex, and contradictory process.

In attempting to retrieve and reconstruct a lived and shared history of women's interventions in the public sphere in Kerala, it covers the regimes of gender disciplining, and the manner in which orthodoxy shaped gender. The literary text had already collected the Kendra Sahitya Akademi Award, the State Sahitya Akademi Award, the Odakkuzhal Award, and the Vayalar Award before it was adapted into a movie by Shyamaprasad in 1999, himself a debutant director at that time. The film won eight state awards, including the award for the best director, best film, best cinematographer, best actor, and best supporting actress. It also

[1] Based on an interview with Shyamaprasad conducted by the author in May 2013.

received the National Film Award for the Best Feature Film in Malayalam in 1999.

There are different temporal frames that *Agnisakshi* the novel, as also its filmic adaptation, encompasses besides a span of more than two decades between the publication of the novel and the release of the movie. The narrative itself is scattered along the early decades of the twentieth century—a period fraught with tensions of modernity and social change in Kerala—as also the rise of the Nationalist movement before the state itself was technically formed, the period of Independence and nation formation, and the post-Independence phase with its ensuing disillusionments. Thus, it roughly marks half a century of the most turbulent and eventful decades in the socio-cultural and political history of Keralam.

This was also a period fraught with important ramifications as far as gender history in the state was concerned. When Antharjanam began writing in the early decades of the twentieth century, gender was a hotly contested terrain, and women's roles in society, as also the division of spheres and ideals of femininity, were all under discussion and negotiation. But by the time these trenchant issues reach the audiences of the film adaptation in the late 1990s, compromises had been affected in what was almost a century of drastic social and political transformation as far as gender and caste in Kerala were concerned. Silences had set in and Antharjanam's analogous, complementary, and often alternate female worlds had become outmoded in what was a gender regressive turn of Kerala's experience of modernity.

Without being overtly caught up in how useful the fidelity approach in studying an adaptation might be, the questions nevertheless have to focus on what happens when a text like *Agnisakshi*, with such radical emancipatory possibilities for women, is translated into the filmic medium where the language of popular cinema is often *not* amenable to feminist politics.

Malayalam cinema has a long tradition of adaptations. In the early years, especially in the 1950s and 1960s, many of the progressive writers in Malayalam, including Thakazhi Sivasankara Pillai, Uroob, Ponkunnam Varkey, and Kesava Dev, whose works were adapted into films or who wrote screenplays for some of the movies, exerted a strong influence in moulding a social realist base for Malayalam cinema. This, however, was gradually dissipated for the more commercial and hegemonic strands that cinema embodies. Shyamaprasad himself is a director who over the years has perfected the art of adaptation, which has become his forte. As an auteur, his thoughts on adaptation of a literary work into film might seem at odds with the aspirations of the literati.

> Most adaptations in Malayalam cinema have focused on the story and plot of the literary piece from which it sought adaptation. Many adaptations, including the most popular ones like *Chemmeen* have focused on retelling the story of the original. However, for me, making a story is not the primary concern of the director. A film-maker is not a storyteller. He or she is one who revels in recreating the experiential world of the original. Therefore, cinema, as a more palpable and sensuous medium, seeks to weave together and entrance the senses. In this attempt to meld the word with images and perceptions, the story itself becomes secondary as far as a film-maker is concerned. It is only a vehicle for transporting the viewer to another aesthetic plane. Thus, it is the language of cinema in which I narrate the tale that is more important to me, not the tale in itself.

These words echo the fact that a director has to be true to his medium more than anything else, and it is not the story to be told, but how it is told cinematically that becomes the hallmark of the auteur's style. This is where issues of fidelity come into play and pose the quintessential dilemma of any adaptation. Fidelity has always been a major concern and issue as far as adaptations are concerned. How far should a film be true to the source literary text? To the question of how faithful he had been to the letter and spirit of Antharjanam's *Agnisakshi* and whether he considered faithfulness to be a requisite at all, Shyamaprasad's words are significant:

A film and a literary work are entirely different. So the task of the director is different from that of an author. A writer's task is conceptual in the sense that s/he is dealing with ideas and thoughts, and has to devise ways of pushing that across. A director has to grapple with more concrete things than that. There is the need to create a real world of images on screen. For this, s/he has to blend the visual and the acoustic, in addition to monitoring other concerns like casting, dialogue delivery, location, setting, and also understanding the technology of the medium. Therefore, a film-maker's commitment cannot be unidimensional to the author. There is the commitment to one's self and art, there is also the commitment to the audience, but most importantly, there is the commitment to the medium itself. While I read and enjoyed Antharjanam's *Agnisakshi*, I could create only my own *Agnisakshi* in the world of cinema. But then, that is a new way of understanding the original.

The film is for the most part faithful to the novel and follows the same structure and sequencing of events. The flashback mode is used throughout, both in the novel and the film. There is also a direct borrowing of Antharjanam's dialogues. The indirect first-person perspective of the novel which is Thankam's is retained in the film's third-person narrative. While the novel offers an explicit critique of patriarchy in Namboodiri illams of the period, the film limits, in more than one way, the exploration of women's social inequality as also the overt challenges that gender posed to social structures in the original text. The film covertly seems to indulge in a neo-conservative mainstreaming of the liberal ideas in the novel, precisely using its locus as a feminist text in Malayalam as also its romance, plot, and characterization to diffuse attention

from the genuine feminist concerns it seeks to echo. The trajec-
tory that *Agnisakshi* the novel traces in its filmic avatar in fact
illustrates the patriarchalization of feminism, a project that has its
roots in the earlier decades of the twentieth century, in the growth
of the reform movement in Kerala under men.

The implicit feminism of Antharjanam's *Agnisakshi* and its
progressive egalitarian foundations are eclipsed and toned down
in the film adaptation where the emphasis is seen to shift subtly
to masculine roles and the notion of 'dharma' in the masculine
context. The polite feminism of Antharjanam with its stress not
on equality of the sexes, but on the complementary roles of men
and women in social life, is further tamed into conciliatory positions where the moviegoers of the 1990s, both men and women,
can be appeased without overtly radical or subversive polemics
coming into play to disrupt or disorient spectatorial pleasure. In
an age when the women's question seemed to have been conve-
niently resolved within the bounds of the modern developmental
nation, and to have almost disappeared from public discourses,
the film seems reluctant to re-dig the grave. Therefore, it seeks to
eschew the multiple axes of women's emancipation and motherhood, both in the private and public domains of life, which the
novel constantly invokes, and chooses to limit itself to the tangled
web of the relationship between Devaki Manampalli and Unni
Namboodiri. Shyamaprasad himself has pointed out that,

> I have retained the basic structure of the story. However, there is a
> shift in focus from the social drama to the intensely individual and
> personal traumas of the characters. I concentrated on the deep love
> between Unni Namboodiri and Tethi, a love that surpasses human
> understanding, and is yet so universal, caught as it is in the bonds
> and bondages of life. Therefore, there is definitely my own touch in
> the style of narration and the treatment, as also in the selections and
> omissions I have made from the original. This is what makes a film

so uniquely different from the novel. At another level, I have also used the story to experiment with the language of cinema, attempting to create new idioms and syntaxes for that language. So, using the medium differently, putting my signature on it was also my concern, not the mere telling of the story of Unni and Tethi.

The language of cinema, as has been researched and analysed, is most often a male language, mirroring the dominant patriarchal conventions and ideologies of an age. How an auteur comes to choose his literary text might point to the fact that the underlying principles of selection might itself undermine the basic ideological premises of the literary text. The male director's words on the choice of an overtly radical feminist text are resonant with such differences:

I have always been fascinated by *Agnisakshi* right from my childhood days. Going beyond the social drama and the period angle of a tale told in the backdrop of a Namboodiri tharawad in the first half of the twentieth century in Kerala and the abysmal changes in the world around it in the wake of the anti-feudal and nationalist struggles, there is nevertheless a story that is essentially timeless and universal. This is the story of transcending love, of one's duties and responsibilities in this world, and of human dilemmas poised between these two. It is about choices or the lack of them, of numerous individual quests—social, religious, spiritual, and emotional. It is also about one's personal failures to sublimate our desires, the existential angst of the human condition, and its predicaments. Therefore, the novel found an early resonance in my heart and I thought it encapsulated many of my experiences and the difficult choices in my life. It also projected for me many of the concerns and issues of the people of my parents' generation. I found myself captivated by this story and it haunted me for years. I mulled over it for a long, long time and thus was born my filmic response and tribute to Antharjanam's classic tale.

It is amply clear that the male director's choice need not necessarily be informed by the imperative to narrate either women's histories or women's subjectivities. Thus, the ideological traces of the male auteur in the film can come into conflict with those of the woman author of the literary text. The male auteur's authority on the celluloid can also function to subtly jettison the female author's concerns in the written text. Thus, Antharjanam's image of the woman as reformer, in direct opposition to the entrenched and received notion of man as reformer, attains an irritant status in the movie through the very casting of Shobhana in the role. She is an actress, whose popular films of the decade invoke an altogether different aesthetic and visual domain. The director, in his attempt to combat the received popular imagery of an all too desirable feminine, does take pains to de-aestheticize her presence and strip her of the signs that are coded for male pleasure. Nevertheless, the star persona triumphs and the director and the actor together seem to fail in bringing Tethi's humanist spirit, radical reformist zeal, and subversive energy to life. Rajit Kapoor, in contrast, as an actor who had successfully deflected visual excesses in his roles and inhabited alternative spaces of filmic representation, seems tailor-made for the role of Unni Namboodiri. The film is unable to offer space for a female gaze which might never have been its object. To the question of whether there was a conscious ideological position that the film sought to represent, or whether it tried to align itself with Antharjanam's political views, Shyamaprasad responds thus:

I did not consciously attempt to bring in any ideological position. With regard to caste, I feel that the Namboodiri background is not the most important or essential aspect of the story, unlike what most critics who stress the community angle, do. In fact, I think the basic story would remain unchanged in a Muslim community too. So. the all too familiar and human conflict between tradition and modernity, irrespective of Nair or Muslim or Namboodiri subject positions coming into play, is what fascinated me most.

A feminist critique of the film would point a finger at the fact that Shyamaprasad has highlighted the loneliness of the woman in the public sphere, thus validating women's confinement in the private spheres of life. However, he strongly and vehemently refutes this charge.

> It depends upon how you would want to interpret it. The female protagonist of the film is lonely by her own choice. One must not forget that Tethi is a very strong character. She does not want to be part of this whole drama of power, but is nevertheless a powerful person. One cannot merely look at her through the lens of gender binaries. She is the one who is vested with action and it is her actions that impel the narrative of the film forward. I chose to omit the chapters of her life where Antharjanam portrayed her in numerous social roles. But the transformation from the Tethikutty silenced inside the confines of her mana to the powerful and ennobling character of Sumitrananda Devi can be interpreted as an act of liberation and empowerment.

However, this omission is a serious one given the fact that it charts precisely the journeys that Tethi makes, the trials and tribulations she faces, and the transformation of the self they effected, through which Antharjanam offers a very strong and trenchant gendered critique of the reform movement in India. In fact, the discontents with nation and religion, the possibilities of motherhood outside the domestic pale, the strategic use of a welfare rhetoric by women to gain entry into the public spaces of the nationalist and reform projects, and the legitimization of such movements come vibrantly alive in these omitted sections. The movie, through its omissions, seems to hold a brief endorsement of the spiritual essentialist foundations of Hinduism. However, the novel's project seems to have been much more complex and nuanced than that. Without rejecting Hinduism, it sought to question its ancient misogynist base, choosing to work within the very same strictures and structures it tried to dismantle or subvert. Many of these early Hindu feminist leaders were able to overcome the hindrances of working within a Hindu society through a strategy of assimilation and accommodation, where separate female institution-building programmes by women were to prove to be the vehicle for the movement for Hindu women's embracing of modernity, by both enabling women to mobilize in pursuit of their own welfare and contributing immensely to the transformation of women's public roles (Anagol 2008: 284).

Much has been said about the male reform project in Kerala in the context of modernity and the manner in which it reformulated both patriarchy and tradition. Antharjanam's *Agnisakshi* seeks to complicate and offer a more nuanced understanding of the 'enlightened paternalism' which was a hallmark of Kerala's reformist ideology. Thus, it was not her Namboodiri father's benevolence alone or Unni Namboodiri's interventions that take Thankam to college, but also her personal ambition and struggle to carve a new self through education. Thankam is a new and gendered sign that radically unsettles the fiefdom of the male household with the Aphan as its feudal lord, administrator, and chief-justice. The *nirahara satyagraha* of fasting and non cooperation that Thankam unleashes within the household in a sense replicates the Gandhian model of resistance. The nation's emancipation and women's emancipation both bring discontents in postcolonial India. Much, much later, Thankam invokes Devaki Manampalli's speech that their legacy of woes, the inheritances of sorrows that she, the mothers, and grandmothers of her generation inherited ought not to be passed on to the younger generation of women. This anxiety is echoed in Devaki's words, as also in the actions that mould her public and private lives. All of this is depicted in the movie too. However, when the story seems to highlight only the relationship between a man and his wife, relegating everything else to the margins, this weight of anxiety and its ideological bearings are neutralized. Thus, a complex historical process is reduced to the myth of the steadfast spiritual masculine and a new cult of the individual feminine whereby the radical gendered spirit invested in social issues in the novel is overshadowed.

Agnisakshi the movie is not a woman-oriented adaptation, while on the surface it might seem to be a largely truthful one. The problem here is also accentuated by the fact that Antharjanam's novel, when read in the post-liberalization era in Kerala, offers possibilities for reading it as both socially progressive and ideologically conservative. The meaning in the film text is produced not solely out of the signs that characters come to represent and the significations of their interactions, but also the contexts and codes in which they are read. In fact, a post-feminist reading can unearth the part of an individualistic and headstrong woman's role in creating her own unhappiness and loneliness through a dysfunctional marriage, thus negating the personal sacrifices and historical functions that Devaki Manampalli undertakes. However, the director's words that she is lonely 'by her own choice', illustrate the hollowing out of meaning from the historical implications of her life and choices. This creates a semantic void into which are filled new events of meaning, as suited to the exigencies of a new age where the women whom Devaki Manampalli sought to 'liberate' have already been tamed by the myth of conjugal domesticity. Thus, a close analysis would reveal how Antharjanam's Devaki, becomes a different signifier in the film through the cinematic image of the 'lonely' and un-domesticated woman. Emptied of its original radical aesthetic, it becomes easy for the film to construct itself as part of the dominant semiological chain of Malayalam cinema and its patriarchal semiotics where woman's bliss is always linked to the confines of the hearth and the home, and Devaki remains as a figure to be sympathized with, but never emulated. So, the movie moves far away from a literary text which could treat domestic self-denial and feminist self-seeking as complementary, and which could offer spiritual solutions along with a rebellious zeal to transform the material and the temporal.

The movie, in contrast, at one level, remains rooted in the simple conventions of the sentimental and the melodramatic, and seeks to revisit a feminine history under the aegis of a spiritual and paternal masculine. The director's comments in a newspaper review subsequent to the release of the movie are very telling. 'Agnisakshi is a spiritual film and the fundamental issue is spiritual identity.' According to Shyamaprasad, Agnisakshi is more than a period film and it tells the story of the transformation of a society caught between two worlds—the past and the future. 'This film was basically made to highlight the plight of the common man and poses many questions about the nature of happiness. It is not about the Namboodiri women alone. It has a sense of timelessness about it,' he says (Shyamaprasad 1999). In another review, Vinu Abraham points out that 'the eternal quest for inner peace, born out of disillusionment in life, is what Agnisakshi is all about,' and argues that 'the film accomplishes a better and detailed treatment of Unni by highlighting the thematic preoccupation of the novel—spiritual quest over materialistic pursuits' (Abraham 1998). The film, which won eight Kerala state film awards, including the best film and best director, came under a lot of fire from left ideologues and critics in Kerala, who accused it of glorifying Indian spiritualism and vindicating Hindutva agendas by deliberately downplaying the radical portions of the novel and accentuating the spiritual (Radhakrishnan 1999).

The movie's point of view and perspective is such that one tends to empathize more with Unni Namboodiri, and the audience tends to sympathize with his character rather than Tethi's. To the question 'Do you think that you were fair to the female protagonist?' Shyamaprasad response is revealing:

> Well, as a male director and a man, my own subject positions and sympathies would be for Unni Namboodiri, more so because I could understand him and align my own choices and dilemmas with his. He embodied for me what I underwent in my life or what my father experienced in his own, a man caught between the past and the future, with a deep sense of commitment to his own destined roles in life. Unable to break free from his past or his lineage and tradition, he is nevertheless the most poignantly modern among all the other characters. He can understand the other and help free the other from the shackles of rituals and habits, while offering himself in sacrifice for the other's freedom.

This answer is an interesting one, given the fact that the movie begins with a dedication, invoking the emotive vocabulary of motherhood where the director dedicates the film to his mother Shantha Rajagopal (1929–1998), thus drawing the informed reader into the same horizon of expectations that the literary original is believed to have attempted. J. Devika has critiqued this process of 'recuperation' of Antharjanam into the liberal humanist canon as the 'Muse of Motherhood' by ignoring the tensions that accompanied her complex rendering of motherhood. Significantly enough, Antharjanam dedicates Agnisakshi to the sacred life of Devi Bahen and all unknown women who made a service of their lives like her, as also her country, her community, and the history of its emancipation. Antharjanam's Devaki, though childless, was mother to many untouchable young children around the illam. There is a poignant description of her relationship with the maid Nani Amma's grandson Unnaman, whose scabs and sores she bathes with oil and soap, whom she feeds with payasam and ada, and for whom she buys books and a slate. These descriptions are compressed to one lacklustre scene in the movie where Devaki feeds the urchin Unnaman some leftover ada, only to be chastised by her mother-in-law and finally laughed at by Unnaman and his companions. The movie also omits the section where years later the grown-up Unnaman, a retired Subedar Padmanabhan Nair, comes to Thankam and begs her to give him Devaki's address because she was the one who made him a man, a human being at whose feet he wishes to fall and weep. 'Here, she is here. In my chest—in my mind. Young mistress's form is imprinted in my life's breath. Amme! I shall look at that and pay my obeisance to her.' This omission blots out the complexity of motherhood that the literary text envisages.

At another level, however, the movie skilfully weaves Antharjanam's project of charting Devaki's journey as one from desire to woman's independence from desire, as also an emancipation from women's function as mirrors for masculine desires. Nevertheless, if Antharjanam's women were desiring subjects who refused to be straitjacketed into male parameters of desire or sexuality, the film, through its visual iconography and the tone and tenor of its treatment, seems to highlight this as a doomed project. It is in this partial or slanted inscription of women's desires, sans a stronger emphasis on its historical and material contexts, that the discursive register of the film seems to privilege dominant discourses that delegitimize such representations. There seems to be a shift in emphasis from the position that female desire can be as fulfilled or as thwarted in the social domain as in the private and domestic to the position that women who 'sacrifice' their lives in the public sphere remain unfulfilled and joyless. This in fact re-emphasizes patriarchal conception of the feminine. Tethi's authority, in the end, seems solely premised on the repression of her womanly desires, and the pinched and harrowed face on screen, the visual structuring of that character, endorse such feminist authority to be meaningless and not to be aspired to by the women in the audience.

However, this kind of a feminist analysis should not miss the fact that normally a movie in Malayalam set in this period could afford endless visual pleasures through a controlling male gaze and an ample scope for scopophilia, which is not the case as far as this film is concerned. Neither the gaze of the camera, nor the gaze of male characters within the film, seeks to transform the woman into an object of desire. The film's visual strategies of representation definitely steer clear of the restrictive/cinematic and characteristic constructions of women. The film gives us numerous brilliant instances of how a director can work around and often circumscribe the conditions of women's representability, and pose subtle challenges to the patriarchal parameters of Malayalam cinema. The aestheticization of the female body is not a concern in the film though the casting of Shobhana does invoke this history of aesthetics and its linkages to the erotic in Malayalam cinema.

The privileging of a Valluvanadan elite Brahminical dialect in many of the films of the post 1990s signify an attempt to write the feudal, Brahminical patriarchy (eased out by the socialist progressive concerns of the earlier decades) back into the representational idiom of Malayalam cinema. However, Shyamaprasad chose Ramapuram, a village where Lalithambika Antharjanam had actually lived. He points out:

I wanted my adaptation to be located in the same place. Thus, my choosing of central Travancore was a conscious decision, though there was a lot of pressure to take it to a Valluvanadan locale, which is a measure of popular taste in Kerala. I particularly wanted the unique ambience of Antharajanam's story to be retained in the film too.

This is no mean task to achieve in a medium such as cinema traditionally steeped in male desires. It is also interesting to note how the movie, in complete conformity with the novel and in direct contradiction to mainstream spectatorial norms, is able to posit masculine domesticity as imbued with a superabundance of qualities, this being especially significant given the rise of hegemonic masculinity in Malayalam cinema by the 1990s. It has been pointed out that Malayalam cinema in the 1990s has been characterized by a re-feudalization of the public sphere and civil society (Pillai 2013a). It has also been suggested that by the 1980s and 1990s, the rhetoric of the popular in an overtly commercial cinema in Malayalam was successful in hitching female fantasies of empowerment and transformation on to the pleasures of consumerism and the allure of commodity, signalling the final blow to the emancipatory possibilities that cinema could hold for the women of Kerala (Pillai 2013b).

The collusive tactics of capitalism, neo-conservatism, and patriarchy together contribute to shaping this rather ironic social phenomenon. It is into this milieu that *Agnisakshi* makes an entry, characterized by a radical disjuncture from this aesthetics and ideology, precisely because it is an adaptation of a literary work credited with the desires for dismantling the patriarchal feudal bases of a society. The film denies the male spectator, groomed in the dominant codes and conventions of popular cinema, any possibility of an activation of scopophilic drives by denying him chance to identify with the narrative hero.

Despite the fact that it does veer away from the dominant codes of cinematic representational traditions in Malayalam, it fails to capture the literary text's attempt to imagine a genealogy of women reformers or highlight positive images of female agency and power vis-à-vis the reform project in Kerala. Antharjanam had herself pointed out in the 'Author's Note' that if the book 'helps the women of the new generation to have a better understanding of their counterparts of the older generation, while persuading the older generation to analyse themselves, and other people to examine the tears and dreams of a bygone age, it will suffice.' Obviously, the function of the adaptation has shifted grounds from this specifically gendered agenda to a more universal cosmic drama of individuals where the milieu, the medium, and auteristic male sensibilities have tamed the progressive feminist aesthetics of the woman author's message in significant ways.

MEENA PILLAI

Works Cited

Abraham, Vinu, 'A Trail by Fire', *The Week*, 18 October 1998.

Anagol, Padma, 'Rebellious Wives and Dysfunctional Marriages: Indian Women's Discourses and Participation in the Debates over Restitution of Conjugal Rights and the Child Marriage Controversy in the 1880s and 1890s', in S. Sarkar and T. Sarkar (eds), *Women and Social Reform in Modern India: A Reader* (Bloomington: Indiana University Press, 2008), pp. 282–312.

Devika, J., *Woman Writing=Man Reading?* (New Delhi: Zubaan, 2013).

Miller, Nancy K., *French Dressing: Women, Men and Ancient Regime Fiction* (New York: Routledge, 1995).

Pillai, Meena T., 'Matriliny to Masculinity: Performing Modernity and Gender in Malayalam Cinema', in K. Moti Gokulsing and Wimal Dissanayake (eds), *Routledge Handbook of Indian Cinema* (London: Routledge, 2013a), pp. 102–14.

———, 'The Celluloid Women of Kerala', *Economic and Political Weekly*, 30 November 2013b, pp. 140–1.

Radhakrishnan, M.G., 'Film Under Fire', *India Today*, 12 April 1999.

Shyamaprasad, 'Agnisakshi, a Spiritual Film', *Indian Express*, 15 January 1999.

Glossary

aarathi	a water rite; literally, worship of an idol with a lamp. Here it refers to the custom of floating a burning cotton wick placed on a leaf in the sacred river and praying for a good husband.
aavanappalaka	a ground-level ceremonial wooden seat
ada	a sweet dish made of rice flour, jaggery, ghee, and honey
adharma	that which is unrighteous
antharjanam	literally, 'anthar' (inside) and 'janam' (persons), it is a name for Namboodiri women meaning 'those who stay indoors'
anthapuram	women's section in a Namboodiri household
aarappoove ... kalu	the sound of cheering (ululation) on festive occasions
Asan	Kumaran Asan, a famous early twentieth-century poet of Kerala
Asoka tree	the grove of Asoka trees, where Sita was held prisoner in Lanka in the Ramayanam
bhagavan	Lord or God; literally, the entity endowed with 'bhaga', the six auspicious attributes of knowledge, omnipotence, lordship, creative power, immutibility, and splendour

Bhagyasooktham	a mantra chanted by Namboodiris every-day for good fortune
bhajanamadhom	a long rectangular room next to the main house in a Namboodiri household where religious rituals and chants are conducted
bhakti	devotion to a personal god. One of the three paths that many might follow to attain salvation, the other two are karma (action) and *gnana* (knowledge).
bhangi	these are scavengers considered untouch-ables
Bharat Mata ki Jai	National Freedom struggle slogan, mean-ing 'Victory to Mother India'
Bhoomi Malayalam	the land where Malayalam is spoken; an exaggerated way of referring to Kerala as the entire earth
brahman	supreme existence; absolute and unchang-ing reality. The source of mind, spirit, and matter.
Brahmaswam	the properties belonging to Brahmins
charka	spinning wheel used by Mahatma Gandhi as a symbol of self-reliance during the Freedom Movement
Chengannattappan	deity of Chengannad temple, Lord Shiva
chittu, cheruthali	symbols of marriage; the bridegroom ties the thali around the neck of the bride dur-ing the wedding ceremony
chovva dosham	flaw in horoscope believed to be caused by the positioning of planet Mars at the time of birth; such a horoscope needs to be carefully matched when arranging

a marriage as it is believed to affect the spouse

darbha	a type of grass grown whose dried form is used in Hindu oblations and sacred rites
deeksha	observance of a year's celibacy, vegetarian diet, non-removal of hair or beard, and daily performance of death rituals in memory of a departed person
Dhanu	a month in the Malayalam calendar (December–January)
embrandiri	a sub-caste of Brahmins who work as temple priests
Ezhavan	one of the lower castes of Kerala, whose ancestors migrated from Sri Lanka and who traditionally earned their living tapping toddy
Ganapathi homam	an early morning puja held in honour of Lord Ganesa before the beginning of any auspicious event
ghosha	the purdah system prevalent among Namboodiris, which forbade women stepping out of their houses without carrying palm leaf umbrellas and shawls to cover their faces and bodies. They were also accompanied by women servants.
gopuram	the gateway to a Kerala temple, built with carvings; normally, there are four gopurams in a temple facing the four directions
gurukula	a house where the disciples of a guru lived together as a family and studied

guru maharaja	a king among teachers; a self-proclaimed guru who has disciples all over the world and is sarcastically referred to by this title
illam	a Namboodiri homestead
kaamam	lust, pleasure, or love
Karkitakam	the last month in the Malayalam calendar
Karkitakavyazham	the destiny concerning married life, assessed through the horoscope based on the stellar sign under which a person is born
karma	action, deed, ritual action, religious observances
karuka	a kind of grass used in yagas, death rituals, and herbal oils
katham	an Indian system of measuring distance, approximately four miles
khaddar	homespun cloth
Kovilakam	the palace of Kshatriya kings of Kerala
Krita Yuga	the first yuga according to Hindu mythology. There are four yugas, the other ones being Treta, Dwapara, and Kali; the present time is supposed to be Kali Yuga.
Kumbhamela	a sacred festival of India when people from every part of the country assemble in Allahabad on the banks of the Ganges to take a dip in the holy river
machu	upper storey of a house
madhom	house of Brahmins
Mahamaya/Mahamaye	the presiding deity of this world, the Goddess of Illusion; the reference is to the Hindu belief that this world itself is

	an illusion and our efforts should be to release ourselves from its power
Mahatma Gandhi ki Jai	a slogan meaning 'Victory to Mahatma Gandhi'
mahilashram	an ashram (abode) for women
mahout	keeper/trainer of elephants
mana	literally means 'house', residence of Namboodiris
mandala	circle, sphere, circumference; an important term in Hindu and Buddhist philosophies to denote the cycle of life
mandaram	*erythrina indica*, the Indian coral tree
mani	bead
mangalyasutram	same as thali
mantrakodi	traditional bridal attire in Kerala
marakkuda	a palm-leaf umbrella Namboodiri women carry to cover their faces
marumakkathayam	the matrilineal system of inheritance prevalent in Kerala among the Nairs, according to which property is passed down through women
moksha	release from worldly bonds
Mooppil Nair	title given by ruler of Kozhikode region, the Zamorin, to the heads of prominent Nair families
mundu	cloth worn around the waist by men and women of Kerala
nadaswaram	a wind instrument (pipe) played at temple festivals
naga sannyasi	mendicant who worships the serpent (snake)

Nair veedu	literally, 'the house of Nairs'; in this book, it is the name of Thankam Nair's tharawad
Nalappadan	short name for Nalappat Narayana Menon, another famous twentieth-century poet of Kerala
nalukettu	a house with a courtyard
namaskaram	salutation greeting
nirahara satyagraha	literally, '*nir*' meaning without and '*ahara*' meaning food, meaning total fast
nirvanam	salvation, release from worldly bonds
Om Namo Narayanaya	'Salutations to Narayana', one of the mantras recited during prayer and worship
oupasanam	the ritual of worshipping the holy fire; a married Namboodiri has to perform this ritual once a day along with his wife
padmasana	one of the positions in yoga in which the practitioner sits cross-legged with each foot on the thigh of the other leg; also known as the lotus position
Panchakshara	the five-lettered sacred chant 'Namassivaya', meaning 'salutations to Lord Shiva'
Patanayar	title conferred on a distinguished warrior
pathala loka	the nether world
pathayappura	double-storeyed building the wealthy occupied
pavizhamalli	sweet smelling white flowers with orange stems
payasam	sweetened milk rice served as dessert at the end of a feast. Here the reference is to the symbol of authority and the significance of the serving of payasam. The new

	bride of the household alone is accorded that honour
pindam	the ball of cooked rice offered to ancestors during the annual death rites ceremony
pitrughat	a bathing ghat on the banks of the River Ganga where rites for ancestors are performed
pradosha sandhya	the time after sunset, twilight
prasadam	items of food offered to the deity and received, sanctified, after the puja
Prasanna puja	a ritual to please the deity
Pulaya	a community of dalits
Puthusseri	a Namboodiri tharawad
Rajarshi	a king (kshatriya) who through his prayers and penance becomes a sage. There are two types of rishis (sages). A brahmin who becomes a sage through his prayers and penance is known as Brhamarshi. The legendary examples of Rajarshi and Brahmarshi are Viswamitra and Vasishta.
Ramarajyam	a phrase coined by Gandhiji to denote an ideal country, this refers to the state of Ayodhya under the rule of Sree Rama, who treated his subjects as equals and gave them freedom, justice, and happiness
Rao Bahadur	a title of honour given by the British to distinguished Indians who were faithful to them
samadhi	deep meditation leading to death by which sages and ascetics attained their final release from life

sambandham	a liason condoned by the social system of Kerala. Namboodiri men lived with Nair women.
sannyasam	renunciation of the world
sannyasi	renunciate
Saptaham	a week-long reading of the sacred book, *Bhagavatham*, narrating the story of Lord Krishna
sastras	scriptural treatises, code of instructions and rules
satyagraha	literally, 'desire for truth', it was a part of the non-violent movement launched by Mahatma Gandhi during the Indian National Freedom struggle
seva	service
Sevashram	the ashram established by Gandhiji during the Indian National Freedom struggle to teach and practice his philosophy of life, which included the principles of living simply, spinning yarn to weave one's own clothes, non-violence, and service to humanity
sidhas	sannyasis, mendicants who have renounced the world
smarthavicharam	the trial for throwing Namboodiri women out of caste and community for sexual impurity. It was conducted according to strict rules, prevalent among Namboodiris till the early years of the twentieth century.

Sraavan	the month of Chingam according to the Malayalam calendar, the month in which Onam festival is held (August–September)
subedar	one of the lower cadres in the Indian army
Swadeshi	of one's own country, in this context, the rejection of foreign clothes preferring instead khaddar made of homespun yarn, woven personally on a charka
Swaraj	one's own country or government; the term is used by Indian leaders such as Balgangdhar Tilak and Gandhi during the Non-cooperation Movement which demanded full freedom for India from the British
Tat twam asi	Sanskrit for 'thou art that', a statement from the Upanishads which assures mankind that the all pervading Brahman is none other than the self/soul
tecchi	*ixora coccinia*, known as the west Indian jasmine, a sacred flower
thampuran	literally, 'master'; members of the Kshatriya clans of Kerala; an overlord/king
tharawad	the joint family households (prevalent in Kerala during the feudal period)
thattu	traditional way of wearing a man's mundu fastened around the waist
thevar	derived from the word 'Devar' meaning god; here the term means Lord Shiva
thirumeni	divine or precious body, it is a respectful term of address for Namboodiri men

thiruvathira	Lord Shiva's birthday and the sixth lunar asterism believed to be the day Lord Shiva met Parvathy. Unmarried women observe a fast to get a good husband, while married women do so for the well being of their husbands
thrimadhuram	three sweet items mixed and offered in worship: coconut scrapings, jaggery, and honey
tirthaghat	bathing ghats on the banks of the River Ganga
Thiruvathira	the day on which women plead with Shiva to bring Kama Deva back to life
Ulloor	short name for poet Ulloor Parameswara Iyer, another famous twentieth-century poet
unnaman	a glutton
Upanishads	the philosophical portion of the Vedas, the most ancient and sacred literature of the Hindus dealing with the nature of man and the universe. They are the source of the Vedanta, Sankhya and Yoga philosophies.
utsavam	temple festival when the idol of the temple is taken out in a procession around the temple
vaisyam	a ritual performed to remember the 101 divine beings where half-cooked rice is offered to them; the ritual has to be performed by a Namboodiri couple—man and wife—together daily

Vanara Platoon	the army of monkeys. A regional group formed by children below the age of sixteen to participate in the Indian National Freedom struggle.
Variar	a community, in charge of collecting flowers and making garlands for the deity in a temple
vavu	the months of the Malayalam year are divided into two parts consisting of fifteen days each according to the ascent and descent of the moon. The fifteenth day of each section is known as *vavu*. There are two vavus in each month—the White Vavu being the full-moon day and the Black Vavu denoting the no-moon day. The vavu day of the month of Karkitakam, the last month in the Malayalam calendar, is supposed to be very important for performing death rites to ancestors, appeasing their departed souls.
Veda mantras	sacred chants (sacred verses) prescribed in the Vedas
Vedanta	philosophy preached by Adi Sankara of Kerala propounding monotheism
Vedas	ancient scriptures containing spiritual knowledge; there are four Vedas—Rig, Yajur, Sama, and Atharva
Veerakumar ki Jai	another slogan meaning 'Victory to the brave son'
Veerakumaran	literally, brave young boy

vilva   sacred peepul tree, known as the Koovalam tree in Malayalam, the leaves of which are used in Shiva puja

Vishu   harvest festival of Kerala; some treat it as the beginning of the Malayalam year. Gifts and money are distributed to all the members of the family.

Viswanathan   ruler of the universe; here the reference is to Lord Shiva

Viswaroopadarsanam   after advising Arjuna before the Maha-bharatam War, Sree Krishna revealed himself as the Cosmic Spirit. This event is known as Viswaroopadarsanam. Literally, 'witnessing the universal spirit'. Cosmic form; omnipresent Vishnu.

yagnam   sacrifice offered to gods

yakshi   imaginary semi-divine being, beautiful and seductive

yogeeswara   god of all yogis; a yogi who has acquired god-like qualities

yogini   a woman ascetic (mendicant)

yogini madhom   the abode or residence of yoginis

yojana   a measure of distance, approximately ten kilometres

yuga   or aeon is a Hindu cosmological term of which there are four: Krita/Satya, Treta, Dwapara, and Kali

About the Author and the Translator

The Author

LALITHAMBIKA ANTHARJANAM, born in 1907 in an important Namboodiri family of Kerala, did not receive any formal education. She was tutored at home in Sanskrit and Malayalam, and acquired proficiency in English and Hindi on her own. Always interested in writing, her first published work was an article on Mahatma Gandhi entitled 'The New Parthasarathy', which appeared in the September 1923 edition of a local magazine called *Sarada*. Her first short story, 'The End of the Journey', was published in the magazine *Malayalarajyam* in 1927. She married Narayanan Namboodiri and had seven children. She was active in the social reform movements of Kerala in the early 1920s. She won the Kerala Sahitya Akademi Award and the National Sahitya Akademi Award for her novel *Agnisakshi*. As one of the early women writers of Kerala who tried to empower women through her writings, Antharjanam is a very important Indian writer. She died in 1987.

The Translator

VASANTHI SANKARANARAYANAN has a doctorate in History from Madras University. Her thesis was on 'Malayalam Cinema: Society and Politics of Kerala', while her MLitt thesis was on the dance dramas of Kerala and their impact on the society and history of the state. She has worked on projects such as the Ramayana Project of Adishakti, a laboratory for theatre arts and research based in Puducherry. She curated the Women's Film Festival, held by InKo Centre, Chennai, and has been on the jury of the International Film Festival of Kerala. Her published translations include *Outcast* (Macmillan India, 1996), *Agnisakshi* (Kerala Sahitya Akademi, 1980), *Retelling the Ramayana* (Oxford University Press, 2005), P. Vatsala's *Agneyam* (Sahitya Akademi, 2006), Kovilan's *Thattakam* (Sahitya Akademi, 2010), and Sarah Joseph's *Vigil* (HarperCollins, 2014). Her articles have also been published in leading dailies such as *The Hindu*, *The Indian Express*, and *The Deccan Herald*.